"You know, I cannot stay here forever."

A smile touched the corners of Gudrun's mouth. "Why not? There is plenty of room and you have certainly made yourself useful. . . . And I believe I know of a man here in town who will come courting as soon as you give the word."

Johanna could feel the blood leave her face. Suddenly she felt lightheaded. "That can never be." Even she could hear the stark despair in the simple words. She shook her head and studied the recent needle prick on the side of her thumb.

"Johanna, I know there are things from your past you want, you need, to keep to yourself. Once I heard Reverend Moen say that a sorrow shared is cut in half. Let me help you with your burden."

"I can't." Johanna shook her head again, slowly as if it were too heavy to move. "I simply cannot."

LAURAINE SNELLING is a full-time writer who has published many books, including those for **Heartsong Presents**. *Song of Laughter*, which marked Snelling's debut as a **Heartsong Presents** author, won the Golden Heart award for excellence in fictional romance.

Books by Lauraine Snelling

Don't miss out on any of our super romances. Write to us at the following address for information on our newest releases and club information.

Heartsong Presents Readers' Service
P.O. Box 719
Uhrichsville, OH 44683

Dakota December

Lauraine Snelling

A sequel to Dakota Dusk

Heartsong Presents

To Colleen L. Reece,
my mentor and friend

A note from the Author:
I love to hear from my readers! You may write to me at
the following address: **Lauraine Snelling**
Author Relations
P.O. Box 719
Uhrichsville, OH 44683

ISBN 1-55748-967-X

DAKOTA DECEMBER

Cover illustration by Randy Hamlin.

PRINTED IN THE U.S.A.

one

"'T'ain't a night fit for man nor beast." Sheriff Caleb Stensrude peered out the window at a world blinded by swirling snow. Sam, a mottled brown and gray cow dog and faithful follower, whined at his master's knee. "What's the matter, old boy, you need to go out?" The dog whined again, his tail brushing the floor in feathery sweeps, then let out a yip as if to agree. "Wouldn't wish that on anyone." The sheriff bent his six-foot-plus frame and fondled the dog's caramel-colored ears. "Well, if you have to go, you have to go. I'll let you out the back so the wind don't sweep you right out to nowhere."

The man whose friends called him Caleb, and everyone else called Sheriff, padded in his carpet slippers through the pantry to the back entry. Once he had been referred to as a tree walking, and even in slippers the description seemed apt. When he cracked open the door, the wind tried to tear it from his hands, "You hurry now, you hear?" He anchored the inside door with one hand and shoved the isinglass-covered screen open just far enough for the dog to scoot out.

"Some way to spend Christmas Eve," he muttered, closing the door. He thought about all the preparations that had gone into the Christmas pageant at the church tonight, all the gifts gathered under the tree, the costumes made and the music practiced. He shook his head. Here he was, all alone, as usual.

Some nights he had fights to break up at the saloon or

someone in his jail needed tending. He'd let old Max out this morning since he'd sobered up—again. Dag had given the old sot his job back at the blacksmith's and the room that went along with it. Good thing. If they'd found Max sleeping in his usual corner north of the saloon, he'd been dead by morning from this cold.

Caleb ran a hand through dark hair now sprinkled here and there with threads of silver. That and a face carved deeply by sun and sorrow made him look older than his thirty-five years. He scrubbed a leathery hand across his square jaw. He guessed he'd hit the sack, soon's that mutt got done with his business.

The wind changed from a whine to a howl, seeking entry and protesting the barriers. The man shivered in spite of his long johns and heavy shirt and pants. He never had liked blizzard weather. Too many living things died.

He cracked open the door again and whistled but the wind blew the sound back down his throat. "Sam, where are you?" He heard a yip and shut the door in disgust. "Can't ya remember which door you went out?" Crossing the room, he could feel the temperature rise the closer he got to the great iron cookstove. He looked longingly at the pot of coffee simmering on the back. Should be strong enough to melt lead by now.

The dog barked again, louder this time. "Hold your horses. You're the one who changed doors." A series of barks pleaded with him to hurry.

Caleb jerked open the door. "Well, get your worthless hide in here." Sam backed off, barking all the while. "This ain't no time for games, git in here." The dog darted off the porch, lost immediately in the swirling blackness. But when Caleb started to close the door, Sam bounded back, his bark demanding now.

"All right, I'm coming." Caleb pushed the door shut but he couldn't silence the wails of the bansheelike wind. He stepped out of his slippers and into his boots, hooking his wool jacket off the coat rack in the same instant. He'd learned years earlier that when Sam insisted on his master following, he always had a reason and a good one at that.

Pulling his hat down tight on his head and wrapping a long woolen scarf around his face, Caleb stepped out into the swirling world. Sam hugged his master's knee, and then moved a little bit forward, leading the way.

They slogged through a hip-deep drift and finally bumped into the fence. Caleb looked back over his shoulder. He could barely see the light from his window. A shape loomed before him.

"Well, I'll be."

Sam yipped and pushed forward. A horse waited patiently, head down, nose almost buried in the snow.

"Help." A weak voice moaned from the horse's back.

Caleb climbed over the gate and reached up in time to catch the woman as she fell. To his astonishment, a small child, hanging on for dear life, fell with her.

"That wind'd do anyone in. Let's get you inside. Can you walk a'tall?"

The woman sagged against him. "Please, take care of my boy."

"Now don't you go frettin', ma'am. I ain't one to leave nobody out in a storm like this, let alone a child." As he talked gently into her ear, he scooped the child under one arm, like he was carrying a sack of wheat, and wrapped the other arm around the woman's waist, half carrying her too. "You stay there, horse, I'll be back."

If he could have figured a way, Caleb would have thrown them both over his shoulders. That would have been much easier as he fought his way through the snowdrifts back toward the light he could barely see. What a night for travelers to be out. Under his breath he thanked the good Lord for bringing them this far and for a dog with a nose and ears to beat all. This wasn't the first time Sam had dragged an injured critter home for tending.

Even the oxlike sheriff was out of breath by the time they all sagged against his front door. While the woman whimpered once in a while, he wasn't sure she even knew she was off the horse.

Afraid to let go of her in case she fell, he finally asked, "Ma'am, can you reach out there and open the door 'fore we all freeze to death?" He tightened his grip on the boy. While he could feel the lad breathing, the poor mite hadn't yet spoken a word.

When Caleb tried ushering the woman in ahead of him, she stumbled and nearly fell. She groaned as her cloak billowed out around her.

Caleb clamped his arm around her again and half-carried her across the room to the rocking chair in front of the cast-iron stove. While she slumped into the chair, he sat the boy down on the rug. Sam licked the child's face and, tail wagging, looked up at Caleb as if asking what to do next.

Caleb knelt in front of the rocker. The woman hadn't even started to untie her cloak. "Please, ma'am, make yourself to home. I'll pour you a cup of coffee and. . ."

At that moment, the woman bit off another moan and slumped forward, hands clasped around her knees. She rocked in place.

"Are you hurt? Do we need a doctor? I—I'm the sheriff here and I learned some about doctoring and that'll just have to do us since we can't go for the real thing in this blizzard." He caught himself. Blathering like an idiot he was.

He sat back on his haunches and stared at the rocking form in front of him. She looked mighty large for such a small woman. *Caleb Stensrude, you idjit, she's breedin', that's what.* He swallowed—hard. "You—you ain't havin' the baby right—right here and now?" He shook his head again. "You ain't—" His voice squeaked. "Not really."

Her soft moan that rose on the end answered him.

"Oh, my. My, oh, my." Caleb rose to his feet, looked at the woman, then looked to thedoor and back again. The wind took that moment to try to blow the house down. No, he wouldn't be going for the doctor.

"How soon, ma'am, how soon?" His insistent voice seemed to penetrate her stupor.

"S—some time yet. Please—my horse. Can't let it die." He had to lean forward to hear her. The child stirred behind him. Jumpin' Josephine, he about forgot the boy.

Sam darted toward the door and yipped. He returned and looked up at his master.

"I know, we have to get that horse under cover before the drift covers the poor critter." He pulled on his ear, hoping the action would provide inspiration. Sam yipped again, as if congratulating the boss on understanding dog talk. He headed for the door and looked over his shoulder. "In a minute, in a minute." Sam sat, momentarily appeased.

Caleb looked down at the boy huddled by the stove. Eyes the color of a summer prairie sky looked up at him, then fear passed through like clouds over the sun. The child's chin quivered and a lone tear slipped down a ruddy cheek.

Caleb felt the stab of the boy's misery clear to his raw-hide-calloused sheriff's heart. He knelt next to the child and with slow gentle hands began to unwrap the boy's tattered red muffler.

"Now, then, let's get you undressed so the heat of that

stove can begin to warm you up." He used the same tone of voice to calm a fractious horse or a bawling calf. It worked on all living things and even some that weren't.

The woman arched in the chair above him, her fingers digging into the rocker arms.

Caleb shot her a glance full of compassion, but at her head shake, he turned back to the boy. "Good, there, son, don't you worry none, your ma is going to be just fine." But when Caleb reached out to check if the flush on the boy's cheeks was from the storm or a fever, the child flinched away. *Someone's been beating the poor little tyke.* The thought made Caleb move even more slowly and carefully. Right away he wished he could meet the low-down rat. Give him a taste or two of his own medicine.

One look at the woman, who was keeping all her misery inside so as not to upset the boy, made him willing to stake his life on the knowledge that it wasn't her. Where was the father? And what were these two doing out on a night like tonight?

"Okay, son, you just keep your things on until I come back from caring for your horse. Do you think you can watch over your ma for those few minutes I'll be gone?" By this time Caleb was beginning to wonder if maybe the boy couldn't hear. Perhaps he was deaf and dumb?

That idea was dashed immediately when the boy slowly nodded, his gaze darting between the woman in the chair and the man in front of him. The eyes looked like they'd seen far too much misery for one so young.

Caleb smiled his most comforting smile and slowly rose to his feet. "Now, you're not to worry, I'll be right back." His promise brought a ghost of a smile to the woman's face but it died under the onslaught of another birthing pang.

Caleb called for Sam and only took time to get his jacket

securely buttoned and hat tied down before he and the dog were out the front door. "I'm counting on you, Sam. You gotta get us back into that house." Sam whined and darted out to where the horse still stood as if frozen.

As the drifted snow had erased all chances of opening the gate, Caleb took the reins and slogged his way around the east side of the house, keeping one hand on the fence when he could locate it. At his side, Sam pushed him back toward the house when the man started to veer too far away.

"I ain't never knowed a northerner bad as this one," Caleb muttered into his muffler. The wind tore the sound away and sent the words to the four corners of the earth almost before the dog could hear them.

Sam yipped and stopped. Caleb brushed the building snow off the brim of his hat and peered through the driving ice pellets. "Good dog." He'd have gone right by the barn, if it weren't for Sam. No wonder people lost their way from the house to the barn in blizzards like this. He leaned his shoulder into the door, rocking it to break loose the ice and snow. When the door finally gave a screech that signalled it was back on its track, he nearly fell into the dark cavern.

The cow lowed from her stall and his horse stamped and nickered a welcome. The sound and fury were muted here in the snug barn where peace reigned supreme. *God knew more than many folks thought when He chose a stable as the birthing place for His Son,* Caleb thought, leading the weary horse into the spare stall and stripping off the harness. This poor woman, whoever she was, didn't even have a saddle. Wonder where she left the wagon? He brushed the snow off the poor beast and felt its ribs in the process. Shaking his head, he dug an old blanket out of the stack of feed sacks and threw it over the horse's back. He poured a scoopful of oats in the feed box, tossed in a forkful of hay, and snagged the water bucket out of his riding horse's manger.

"He needs it worse 'n you," he said, giving the rangy gray gelding an extra stroke and a slap on the rump.

Knowing he'd rather stay in the peaceful barn than face the ordeal ahead in the house, nevertheless, when all was done to his satisfaction, he pulled the door closed against the still howling wind. He grabbed the rope he had strung from the barn to the house for instances such as this and pulled the muffler up clear to his eyes. A drift had even buried one of the posts that held the rope up. Sam stayed right beside him through the accidental detour and got his master back on track.

After what seemed like hours of fighting the elements, Caleb stopped on the porch and filled his arms with wood for the fire. Good thing he'd spent a few days splitting and stacking firewood. Thank the good Lord for His blessings of a warm house, snug barn, and food to last out the blizzard. Not much chance anyone would be calling for the sheriff tonight. He had enough problems in front of him. "Lord above, give us a special helping of Your Grace this night as I help this poor woman bring her baby into the world." He paused long enough to brush some of the snow off and let himself into the kitchen.

Sam shook all over and trotted over to the stove where the boy still sat huddled in his coat. The dog nosed the child's face as if making sure he was all right, then curled up right next to him.

Caleb dumped the wood in the woodbox and turned to study the woman. She lay back in the chair, eyes closed. Her lashes seemed to him like dark feathers on skin so clear the blue veins under her eyes were unnaturally pronounced. He didn't want to think about it but the blueness could be traced to another source. Another spasm caused her to bite her lower lip and dig her fingers into the chair arms. When it passed, she looked up at him. She tried to smile but the effort proved too much and her eyelids drifted closed.

Caleb shifted his attention to the boy. He lay sound asleep, his head now pillowed on Sam. The dog wagged the tip of his tail, careful not to disturb his precious charge.

"Good dog." The big man removed his coat and hat, hung them on the rack by the door, and pulled off his boots at the jack. Even without the storm, this promised to be a long night.

Since there was no heat in the bedroom, Caleb made a pallet out of quilts and lay it by the stove. He put a pot of extra water on to boil, knowing there was plenty of hot water in the reservoir too. Tenaciously, he kept his mind on each task. He didn't want his thoughts to race ahead to the birth itself and throw him into sheer panic. No different than with a cow, he reminded himself. Nature knew what to do about birthing whether people did or not. His hands shook when he tore an old sheet into wide strips, and then proceeded to fashion a baby blanket and diaper-sized squares from the remnants.

When he tried to whistle "Away in a Manger" his pucker wouldn't cooperate. He licked dry lips and hummed under his breath instead.

"Now, ma'am." He scrubbed a weathered hand over his chin. "I can't keep calling you ma'am like this. I know you got a name. I am Caleb Stensrude, sheriff of this little spot in the road called Soldahl, North Dakota."

He waited.

Her eyes darted from side to side, like a mouse caught in a feed barrel searching for an escape. She started to say something and grunted instead as the pain rolled over her, squeezing her entire being. When it passed she panted and forced out her reply through clamped lips. "I—I am Johanna—Carlson—and this is my son Henry. I—we thank you for taking us in like this." She closed her eyes and wet her dry lips. "I am sorry to be such a burden and on Christmas Eve, no less."

He immediately wished she'd open her eyes again. Looking into them had been like finding a deep pool in a clear stream, the kind of pool where trout hid, waiting for a unsuspecting fly to dimple the surface. He'd seen pools like that, clear and full of promise, back in Wisconsin before he came west.

He gave himself a mental shaking and went back to gathering the supplies he thought he might need before this night was over. All the while his hands kept busy, and his mind continued pounding on heaven's door for protection for all of them in the hours ahead.

"You think I could put Henry in my bed to sleep? Poor lad is all tuckered out."

Johanna answered on a sigh. "Yes, if we can hear him if he calls. He suffers some from nightmares."

"We can and I'll tell Sam here to stay right beside him. A good dog lyin' alongside a body makes the dark easier to bear."

"Thank you, Sheriff."

Caleb started to correct her. He didn't much care for the title when it came from her lips.

He wondered how Caleb Andrew Stensrude would sound with her soft—was it just a hint of Norsk?—accent. What was the matter with him, thinking things like that? For all he knew, she was married and her husband. . . . No, he felt sure there was no husband in the vicinity. No man would leave his wife and son out in weather like this. Especially not in her condition.

He picked up the sleeping Henry and, nodding for Sam to come along, walked into the bedroom back of the parlor. He peeled back the covers with one hand as he lay the child gently on the bed. The boy stirred but instead of waking lay limply against the pillow. While Caleb removed the boy's boots worn so thoroughly the leather was split clean through, Sam leaped up on the bed and, after a glance to his master for permission, curled himself into the boy's side. Caleb tucked in the covers and laid a hand, surprisingly gentle for one so large, on the boy's forehead to check for fever.

"You take good care of him, dog, you hear me?" Sam thumped his tail and laid his muzzle on the child's chest.

Back by the stove matters had taken a turn for the worse. Johanna clung to the arms of the chair, trying to regain her feet.

Caleb leaped to her assistance. "Please, you could fall and hurt yourself."

"Have to lie down," she panted. "The baby is ready to come—n—o—w." The final word turned into a wail. She collapsed on the pallet and continued to pant, the contractions seeming to roll over and through her body with ruthless intensity.

When Caleb checked to see how she was progressing, he literally caught the baby as it slithered onto her soaked petticoats.

"Oh, dear God above, now what?"

The infant let out a yell fit to scare the wind howling in the chimney.

"Well, will you listen to that." Caleb cradled the squalling red baby in his cupped hands and stared at her as if he couldn't believe his eyes. He looked up to see Johanna watching him.

"You have a baby girl, ma'am, Miz Carlson. And she sure does have a hearty pair of lungs. All the rest of her appears intact, too."

"You—you need to cut the cord."

"All right." He looked around for a place to lay this now quiet mite.

"Put her here, on my chest." The woman patted the spot.

"But you'll get all—I mean—well, she's a bit messy, you know."

"If'n you got a clean towel, lay that down first since my dress ain't the cleanest." Was that a twinkle he saw in her eye?

The sheriff felt his confidence return. "'Course. That's what I was thinking to do."

Laying the baby face down on the woman's belly, he took the bit of rag he had torn and tied the cord off and severed the membrane. Now the little one was on her own. As if unhappy with that situation, she squalled again, already turning her head in search of sustenance.

Johanna groaned again as another spasm racked her body and expelled the afterbirth.

"Good. There, there, ma'am. You are doing just fine." Caleb cleaned up the mess as he spoke, doing all in his power to help his patient and yet not embarrass her. There should have been another woman present in this intimate task, or at least the doctor.

Poor lady would probably never be able to look him in the eye again. At the thought, his heart clenched as if caught in a huge hand. Must be he was mighty lonely this Christmas night to be worrying about whether this poor woman would want to see him again or not.

Calling himself all sorts of names, he brought out the strips of old sheet he'd torn up, folded a square patch to put over the baby's umbilical cord, and tied it in place. Next he folded a larger square around the infant to keep her warm and laid her in the crook of her mother's arm.

"How about if I clean her up later?"

Johanna nodded. "Sheriff, that would be just fine. You've done far more than you'll ever know." In spite of the weariness that pulled at her eyelids, she smiled up at the man kneeling beside her.

"She's so beautiful." Caleb touched the tiny fingers curled into a fist. The baby opened her hand and wrapped her fingers right around the end of his. At that moment Caleb lost his heart, giving it over to that bit of humanity whether he wanted to or not.

"I believe we should call her Angel," he whispered as if anything louder would break the spell. "That is, if'n you want to."

"I believe that would be right fine."

"Angel what? She needs more of a name than that."

But the woman and child had both fallen asleep, breathing peacefully in the lamplight.

"Well, I'll be." It was some time before Caleb Stensrude could tear himself away from the picture on the pallet. As he wrapped his tired body into a quilt, he whispered into the night, "Dear God, please let me hear if one of them needs me."

two

He awoke with a start.

The room had turned chilly, no doubt fueled by the draft that sneaked across the floor and worked its way in through the quilt he'd wrapped around himself. The kerosene lamp he'd left with the wick on low now flickered feebly, the wick burned down too far.

What had awakened him?

Caleb threw back the covers and, after getting to his feet, made his way to the table, first to wind the wick higher and then to the stove to add more wood. The harder he tried to be quiet, the more the stove lids rattled and the wood banged against the sides of the fire box before flaring in the remaining coals. As the wood caught, he set the round lids back in place and dusted off his hands.

He listened and nodded. That's what it was, the quiet. The wind no longer moaned and whistled at the eaves, demanding entry like a frothing beast. He looked over at the pallet of quilts where mother and babe slept. Rubbing a calloused hand across his forehead, he thought back to the birthing. Gratitude for the ease of it made him clamp his jaw. What if the baby had been a breach birth or born dead? He shook off such morbid thoughts. That was over and done with. Now he only had to deal with a newborn baby, a woman who looked like she needed more than one night's sleep and a month of good feeding, and a little boy who wouldn't—or couldn't—talk.

Might be easier to take on a bunch of cowboys at the end

of a long trail ride. The thought made him rub his forehead again. What was he gonna do with them? They couldn't stay here, in the house of a widower, without chaperones. Why, if Mrs. Jacobson down at the Mercantile got wind of this tidbit, she'd hang them out to dry in every home in Soldahl. He wouldn't be able to walk down the street without people whispering behind their hands. And what would this do to Mrs. Carlson? No, this wouldn't be the way to introduce her to the community.

Besides, he had no time for a boy and a baby.

At that thought the baby mewled, a tiny sound that called forth every caring instinct he never knew he had. The utterly helpless cry flew straight across the room and, like an arrow, sank into his heart.

Angel, that's what he'd named her. If the little family moved on he would probably never see her again. He wouldn't watch her grow and laugh and play.

He cleared his throat.

"I am awake, Sheriff, there is no need for you to try so hard to be quiet." The soft voice came through the dimness.

"Yes, ma'am. Is there anything I can get for you?"

The mewling changed to whimpers.

"No, thank you. I will nurse this one here and. . ."

"Does she need dry diapers?"

"Yes, I'm sure she does. Have you some here?"

"Just pieces of that sheet. She's wearing part of it now." Caleb left his place by the stove and fetched the folded pieces of cloth. He handed them down to the woman who had rolled on her side. "You need some help?"

"Yes."

He could tell the admission cost her dearly. He knelt beside the pallet and, unwrapping the sheet turned blanket, removed the soiled article. Then, after refolding a small square, he tucked it between the twiglike legs and wrapped the baby tightly in another piece of sheet.

"You do that like you've done it before." She shifted her gaze from the bundled baby to the man who now sat back on his haunches.

"Not much different than wrapping a package in brown paper." He resisted the urge to touch the questing rosebud mouth with the tip of his finger. "I'll let you be now." He got to his feet. "You need anything now, you just call out. Hear?"

"Yes, Sheriff."

Caleb crawled back into his quilt to give her the privacy he sensed she needed. The rustling of moving bodies and fabric, punctuated with Angel's demand for food, painted pictures on the backs of his eyes. Pictures of Harriet and the times she'd nursed their sons. Pictures of warmth and love. Even at only a few hours old, Angel nursed with determination. He could both hear and feel it. Caleb folded a hand under his head and kept a sigh to himself.

What a Christmas Eve this had been. Christmas morning was only a few hours away. Surely he had something in the house that might be given as a present to the little boy. He wracked his brain.

No toys. No child-sized clothing. All the gifts still lay under the tree at the church so he hadn't even an orange or a candy cane. He turned to his other side. Some of the townsfolk had dropped off presents of food—a ham, chocolate cake, julekake—to thank him for helping them at one time or another. He catalogued the things he had set in the pie safe. All well and good but no gift for a small boy who looked as if he hadn't had much in his young life.

Father, Caleb prayed, *You sent me these wanderers so now*

*I have an extra request. Since they are here, could You pro-
vide a gift for the little fellow? You know I can't come up
with an idea. And while I'm at it, thank You again for keeping that little Angel and her mother safe. Please keep Your
angels guard over us. You seem to like babies born at this
time of year. Amen.*

He lay snug in his quilt, one of those that his wife Harriet
had made so lovingly. Strange how something she made
could still bring him such comfort, let alone warmth.

As soon as first light turned the blackness outside to dark
gray, he rose and added wood to the fire. After pulling on
his boots and bundling up, he then headed for the barn to do
his chores. He always thought better in the barn anyway.

With his head butted up against the cow's warm flank and
milk streaming into the pail, he mulled over what to do next.
By the time he'd poured milk in the pan for the barn cats,
fed the chickens, tossed hay into the horse and cow man-
gers, and refilled the animals' drinking buckets from the
barrel of water, he knew what he had to do. What time would
Gudrun Norgaard be ready to offer him coffee and advice?
Even if it were Christmas morning, she always knew what
to do with angels and strays. This wouldn't be the first time
he'd conferred with her and, knowing the way of the world,
it probably wouldn't be the last.

He caught himself whistling on his way back to the house.
The rooster finally got himself awake enough to greet the
dawn that still struggled to be seen through the lowering
clouds. The temperature had dropped along with the wind
but at least the blizzard was over for now. He could still
smell snow on the breeze along with wood and coal smoke
as the people of Soldahl fueled up their fires for breakfast.

He had someone to cook breakfast for too. That thought
lent a spring to his step that seemed positively un-Caleblike

had anyone been watching.

Sam met him at the door and scooted outside as soon as he opened it. By the time Caleb put the milk pail on the table, the dog yipped to come in. "Taking your duties with that little fellow mighty serious, aren't you?" The man only had to hold the door a second before the dog was through and, with a quick tail wag and a whine over his shoulder, Sam headed for the bedroom.

Caleb nodded in approval. Sam was smarter than he gave the critter credit for, and that was saying something. He left the pantry along with his boots and coat and padded into the kitchen. The coffeepot gurgled on the back burner. The floor where the pallets had been laid was swept clean. And there wasn't a human in sight.

They're gone! The thought caught him like an unexpected blow from a barroom brawler. But the sight of the boy's ragged muffler strewn across the horsehair sofa's arm eased his anxiety. She must be taking care of the boy.

Should she be out of bed? What did all this effort cost her?

On the wall by the front door, the carved walnut clock, his only legacy from his grandfather, chimed seven times. He'd go talk with Gudrun as soon as he fed his guests. Maybe she had some flannel or something that could be turned into diapers for Angel. Maybe Mrs. Olson would know where some necessary things would be. Between Gudrun Norgaard, the grand dame of Soldahl, and Mrs. Olson, her dedicated housekeeper, they knew about everything that went on in these parts.

His mind played with the words as, under his breath, he whistled the opening bars of "Away in the Manger."

"You sound in a joyful mood." Her soft voice startled him so he clattered the black-iron skillet on the top of the stove.

"Oh, I am at that. Merry Christmas and good morning."

He looked at her more closely. "Are you sure you shouldn't be lying down? I mean, like, you had that baby not very many hours ago." His fluster had attacked his tongue. Why should an itty-bitty woman like this make him stutter? When he faced a gang of drunken field hands he felt like he could conquer the world!

"I—I thank you for your concern, but me and mine, we must be on our way as soon as possible."

"On your way! Woman, you just had a baby, we just had a blizzard. Looks to me like another is right on its heels and it's cold enough out there to freeze spit before it leaves your mouth." Caleb rattled the pan and shoved it off to the side. "'Sides, I'm just readying up some breakfast for us. You do think you could stay long enough for a meal?" He could hear the sarcasm but seemed unable to stem it. What in thunder was so all-fired important she had to run off like this?

He took a slab of bacon out of the pie safe and eggs from the pantry and assembled his fixings on the table. He started to cut the bacon and instead turned to the stove. Fetching two mugs off the warming shelf, he poured coffee into both and pointed at the rocking chair. "Sit."

She sat.

He handed her a mug and, wrapping both of his hands around his own, stood by the stove, lightly resting his haunches on the edge of the reservoir. "Thank you for making the coffee."

"You are welcome." Her voice came, as wooden and stiff as long woolen underwear off a winter clothesline.

"Now the way I see it. . ."

"What makes you think you see it at all?"

"Excuse me for sayin' this, but you show up on my doorstep in the middle of a blizzard, have a baby on my floor. . ."

"It wasn't exactly on your floor." She threw back her shoulders almost indignantly.

You are handling this like a hard-headed Swede. Caleb could hear his father's voice as if he were right in the room.

Caleb figured he'd better listen. "Now, I meant no offense, ma'am, but please, let me help you. The Good Book says to welcome strangers, might well be angels unaware."

"An angel I'm not." A spring thaw might be setting in.

"No, but that little one is and you'd sure be risking her life if you set out now." He spoke gently, like he did to all wounded and desperate creatures. Man, she sure could manage to rile him up. He studied the conflicting emotions as they drew maps on her face. When she lifted her chin and met his gaze, he knew she'd made a decision. He sure as heaven hoped it was the right one.

three

"I will stay."

Caleb felt his breath leave in a whoosh. He hadn't been aware he was holding it. To cover his flash of jubilation, he raised the mug to his mouth and took a swig. Even after being out of the pot this long, the rich coffee scalded the back of his tongue. He could feel the heat clear to his gullet.

"Are you sure this—my being here with my family—will not cause you hardship?"

"No, not at all." A vision of Mrs. Jacobson in full sail flashed across his mind. Dear Lord, forgive this slight untruth. "Not at all." He returned to his bacon slicing and carefully laid the slabs in the pan, making sure the slices were evenly spaced. As if that mattered. When the bacon sizzled to his satisfaction, he sliced the bread and proceeded to set the table.

Finally, when he looked over at Mrs. Carlson, she was resting peacefully in the chair, eyes closed, her cheeks two red circles on an otherwise pale face. Mayhap he should stop by and see the doctor on his way back from Gudrun's. Wouldn't hurt to have him check her and the baby out.

Where was her husband? If she'd been a widow, wouldn't she have said so? Where had she come from and how long had they been on the road? The thoughts sizzled through his mind, like the grease that danced in the frying pan.

The click of Sam's toenails alerted him. Caleb looked up to see Henry stop in the doorway. A wet path down one cheek gave mute testimony to the tears shed, but not a sound had come from him. Caleb knew he would have heard the child crying. Sam whimpered.

Mrs. Carlson jerked alert in her chair. "Oh, Henry, come here." She reached her arms out to him. Giving the man standing at the stove a wide berth, the slender child rushed into her arms.

"I ain't goin' ta bite you, son." Caleb kept his voice easy. That wasn't just shyness he recognized in the look the boy threw him. That was out and out fear. Nigh on to terror. "There's a slop bucket out on the back porch so's he don't need to use the privy. I ain't shoveled a pathway out there yet."

"Thank you, I found it earlier." She kept her arm wrapped around the boy, as if to shield him.

"There now, you can come up to the table to eat or I can bring it to you there." Caleb took a plate off the warming ledge and slid two fried eggs onto it. He added bacon, wished he'd thought of frying the leftover potatoes, and looked up at his guests.

Henry was glued to his mother's shoulder, staring at the plate of food as if he'd never seen such bounty.

"Can you manage the chair? I can put a pillow on it." He put the plate down and did as Caleb suggested without waiting for his mother's approval.

When they were both seated at the table, the boy now on her lap, Caleb fetched butter and jam from the pantry, along with forks and knives. Somewhere he knew he had napkins but for the life of him, he had no idea where.

When they looked up at him, as if asking permission, he waved them on. "Go ahead, eat up whilst it's hot."

"Do you not say grace?"

"'Course. But mine ain't done yet—oh all right." He slid into his chair. "E Jesu navn, gor ve til brod. . . ." He intoned the Norwegian words his mother had drilled into his soul when he was but a young sprout at the table. At the "Amen" he rose and returned to the stove. Good thing he'd shoved the pan back or it would surely be smoking them out of house and home.

Sam took his place at the boy's feet.

Caleb looked over just in time to see a small hand sneak a bit of bacon to the dog. The boy looked up in time to see Caleb watching him and his face went deathly white. He hid his face and as much of the rest of him as possible in his mother's shoulder and shook his head when she offered him another bite of bread.

Caleb finished dishing up his own food and took his plate, along with the coffee pot, to the round oak table. "Can I warm yours up?" At her nod, he poured the dark liquid into both of their cups and eased into his seat. He felt the way he did when out hunting deer, as if the slightest sound would send the game leaping away, to vanish in the woods. Struggling to find words to say, he decided instead to satisfy his stomach. He felt like he hadn't eaten for a week. All the while he called himself every name in the book and a few new ones he'd just come up with. What was the matter with him? Only that he had let a woman like this and her shy-unto-tears son make him uncomfortable in his own house.

"Thank you, Sheriff. That was very good." Mrs. Carlson neatly placed her knife and fork across the plate. "And now if I can prevail upon you just one more time." He nodded at the question in her eyes. "Could you please bring my horse around? We must be on our way."

"Lady, if that don't beat all." Caleb started to slam his hands on the table but one look at the terror-stricken child and he toned his voice down. He shoved his hands in his waistband and tilted back in the chair.

He started again, forcing his voice to sound calm and soothing. "I have to tell you, I cain't do that. You and these children would freeze to death before you got five miles out of town, what with the drifts and all. That north wind would blow right through you and I know you love your children more than to submit them to that." *What are you running from?* He ached to ask the question, but while he had grilled many a suspect, he couldn't get the questions from his mind to his tongue.

"But we cannot stay here." She looked at him, across the child's head, one of her hands stroking the boy's hair. "You have been more than kind, you have saved our lives, but I know what life is like in a town. People talk."

"Not about this sheriff they don't." He knew she was right, that's why he'd been planning on discussing this with Gudrun.

"Sheriff, I'm surprised someone hasn't been at your door already."

As if on cue, Sam let out a yip and rose from the floor at the boy's feet. A growl and then a bark announced the visitor before the knock on the door.

"Good dog." Caleb sent the woman a look promising further discussion, then made his way to the door.

"Merry Christmas, Elmer." But at the look on the man's face, Caleb went no further. "What's wrong?"

"There's a man been shot, Sheriff. You gotta come quick."

"Well, I'll be, can't people forget their squabbles on Christmas?" Caleb muttered as he rammed his feet in his boots and thrust his arms in the sleeves of his coat. Just before grabbing his hat, he turned to the woman by the stove. "You wait here."

Immediately chagrined at the way he snapped an order at her, nevertheless he followed his deputy out to the gate, plowing through the drifted snow and walking right over the fence on a frozen drift. Soon the entire town would know there was a strange woman over to the sheriff's house. Elmer Hanson was a good man with a loose lip and nothing Caleb did seemed to make a difference. And Lord knew, he'd tried.

Caleb settled his Stetson farther down on his head, wishing he had grabbed the woolen billed one with ear flaps. A day like today was no time for a Stetson. "Any idea what happened?"

"Nope, none. He was laying by the livery, half-covered by drifted snow. Looks to been there quite some time."

"How you know he was shot?"

Elmer turned and cocked one eyebrow at his boss. "Has a hole in his chest. Tried to stop the bleeding with a rag. Didn't look to do much good."

"You s'pose he got lost in the blizzard?" His breath blew out in a cloud of steam. While the sun was trying to separate the clouds, it hadn't succeeded as yet.

"Maybe he was looking for the doc and just didn't get that far." Elmer slapped his hands together to improve the circulation. "Man, it's cold still. He wouldn't a laid there long without freezing to death, if the bullet didn't get him."

They stepped up onto the boardwalk, making faster time when they didn't have to plow through snow. Smoke rose from the hotel chimneys but the Mercantile, the drug store, and Swenson's barber shop all wore their Sunday sleepiness. Even the saloon was closed in honor of the holiday. No one else had ventured out, leaving the street blanketed in pure white.

"You want me to get the doc?" Elmer sniffed, then hawked and spit.

"No. Why bother him if the man's dead for sure? We can put him on a wagon and take him to Sorensons. Even undertakers have to work on Christmas. Terrible." They left the boardwalk, turned the corner at the feed store, and stopped just outside the doors to the livery.

Caleb could hear Will Dunfey, Dag Weinlander's apprentice, caring for the livery animals. The boy lived in a snug room in the barn off the blacksmith shop.

"You talk to Will?"

Elmer shook his head. "I told you, I came straight to your house." He pointed to the body lying on the other side of a drift. "There he be."

Caleb dropped down to his haunches. Everything Elmer had said looked to be true. "You ever seen him before?"

"Nope, never."

Caleb studied the face frozen in death. Swarthy, black beard, big nose. Caleb thought he looked like the gypsies he'd once chased out of town. But long dead, that was for certain. "No trace of a horse or wagon?"

Elmer looked pained. "Sheriff, that blizzard wiped out anything and everything. You know that."

"You think he was dumped here?"

Elmer shrugged. "Whyn't we just haul him over to Sorensons and go on home. I shoulda done that without bothering you." He gave the sheriff an appraising look. "Who's that woman at your house? I din't know you had company."

"Just a stranger who got caught in the storm." Caleb strode off around the corner of the building. "I'll get Will to harness us a horse and wagon."

An hour had passed by the time they got the body delivered and Will dropped the sheriff and Elmer back at the sheriff's office tucked into a corner of the county courthouse, one street off Main. Elmer clanked the glowing cinders in the potbellied stove and added more coal.

"What you goin' to do about him—the body I mean?"

"Guess we'll just ask around if anybody knows of him. Maybe put it out on the wire, a description and all. Wait and see if anyone inquires about him. Can't bury him 'til the spring thaw, that's for sure." Caleb took the proffered cup of rotgut that in Elmer's mind passed for coffee and added two spoonfuls of sugar. When he was on duty the coffee was drinkable, black the way he liked it, but his deputy made a pot and boiled the life out of it, then set the pot to simmer. The only good thing about the drink this morning was its heat. Even the steam felt good when he raised the doctored brew to his lips.

A picture of Mrs. Carlson sipping from her breakfast cup flashed through his mind. What if she took it in her mind to leave?

"Think you can hold down the fort today? Shouldn't be too much going on." Caleb forced himself to stand still when all he wanted to do was head for home.

"Can't think why not. You don't mind if I go to church though?" Privately, Caleb thought his deputy's devotion to the Lord had more to do with the younger sister of Mrs. Jacobson, who was visiting for a time. Mrs. Jacobson and her husband ran the Mercantile, or rather she ran the store and him too. But Mary Louise had caught the eyes of most of the town's bachelors. Not only was she pretty but she was of marrying age and not spoken for.

Caleb had been forced to point her in another direction when she set her bonnet for him. Why, he was old enough to be her father. And he told her so.

"You go on to church and have a Merry Christmas, Elmer." Caleb nodded and left before the young man could ask the question buzzing behind his eyes. Asking him to keep his mouth shut about the sheriff's guest would have just made matters worse.

When Caleb reached Main Street again, he debated whether to stop at Gudrun's, the doctor's, or just head on home. He looked up the street to see smoke coming from the Lutheran church's chimney. Mighten be he should talk to Pastor Moen instead of Gudrun. He kept abreast of the town events nearly as well. So often people in trouble called on the Lutheran pastor, and with good cause. John Moen took exemplary care of his flock, including any strangers, strongly believing and preaching the joy of hosting angels unawares.

Like the Angel sleeping at his house. Caleb started home, but turned off the street to Doc's anyway. Mrs. Carlson had looked a mite feverish. As he firmly believed, better safe than sorry.

Dr. Harmon himself answered the door. When Caleb explained the situation, Doc nodded, his mouth full of Christmas bread, and shoved his arms into the coat sleeves.

"I'll be back in a few minutes," he hollered over his shoulder. Grabbing the black leather bag he kept by the door, he followed in Caleb's footsteps. "Shoulda gotten out here earlier and shoveled this, but Mrs. Abramson had a bad attack last night. Thought I'd never get home. When I finally staggered in the door, all I wanted was my bed."

Caleb nodded. "You went out in that blizzard?"

"No, they came for me just about the time it quit." Doc looked up at his anxious friend. "What's the rush? You said she seemed fine."

"Just a feeling I have. First that fellow dead by the livery and now. . ." Caleb shook his head. Long ago he'd learned to trust his feelings that something wasn't quite right. They kicked the snow off their boots against the front porch post.

Tail wagging, Sam met him at the door.

But the house was empty.

four

Leave it to a woman not to obey orders.

"Maybe she's in the other room." Doc pointed in the direction of the bedroom.

Caleb strode through the parlor, knowing that his search was in vain. The house had that empty smell, even though she couldn't have been gone long. And Sam hadn't left that boy's side since they arrived. Sam took his charges seriously.

"No, nothing."

"You sure you didn't dream this woman up?" Doc grinned at his friend but quickly snuffed out the humor. The sheriff's face made it clear what he thought of the joke.

"How'd she get away so fast?" Caleb rubbed his upper lip. "Sorry to have brought you out. Think I'll saddle up and follow her. With no one else out on the streets, she'd leave an easy trail."

"Bring her to my house when you find her. Be better for her there, and for you too. You know those jokers'll be all over your hide and the women too. Martha and I'll take care of her 'til we figure what else to do."

Why did that suggestion make him want to grit his teeth? Caleb leaned down to scratch the top of Sam's head. The dog whined and, after a quick finger lick, headed for the back door.

"That's the way all this started," Caleb muttered. "You and your need to find a tree." He turned on his way and waved at the doctor. "See you soon, I hope."

As soon as he opened the back door, the dog lit out over the snow as if wolves were on his heels. Over the fence and the drifts, straight on a beeline for the barn.

Caleb knew enough to follow, although the knee-high snow slowed him somewhat. Sam had his gray nose pressed to the crack in the barn door, his tail whipping from side to side. A whine suggested in no uncertain terms that his master ought to pick up his feet a whole lot faster.

"I'm coming. I'm coming." Sam darted through the crack before Caleb, his shoulder against the door, pushed it full open. In the same moment, he realized there were no horse tracks leaving the barn door. The snow was so packed against the door, it had only been opened enough to let one person in. Just as if he'd left it after milking and caring for the animals. Tracks went in, but no tracks came out.

"Doc! Doc Harmon!" He yelled as loud as he could.

"Coming."

With that Caleb entered the barn, fear and anger waging a war in his soul. Whatever possessed her to start out like this? She hadn't appeared daft but now he was beginning to wonder. He blinked in the dimness but didn't let that slow him down.

"What do you think you're doing?" He leaped forward to catch her as she fell.

"Take care of Henry, please." Her voice quavered and her eyelids fluttered. "I—I'm sorry."

"You should be." Caleb felt like shaking her. How could she be so stubborn as to put herself and her children in such danger? She'd gotten the bridle on her horse and an old saddle blanket in place. A saddle, not his good one, stood on its horn beside the stall post. Was she going to steal it? He shook his head. But of course, she couldn't reharness the beast.

"How bad is she?" Doc Harmon knelt beside them.

"I don't know." Caleb looked around again. Henry huddled in the corner of the stall, clutching the quilt-wrapped baby in his thin arms. The two were almost invisible in the darkness of the stall. Sam scooted past his master and, after a quick swipe of the boy's nose, wriggled into the straw beside him. Caleb's horse snorted and stamped his feet. The cow grunted as she lay down again. Here in the barn all seemed so peaceful, so normal. Except for the woman with the bright spots of fever on skin so pale you'd think you could see right through it.

She moaned softly and turned her head from side to side.

"We better get her to my house where my wife can nurse her. I'd guess she's ended up with an infection and, traipsing out here to the barn with two young'uns, well, I don't know. Sometimes you just wonder." He took her wrist between his thumb and fingers and counted her pulse. "You suppose something frightened her?"

"She was pretty determined to get on the road. Either she is running from something or has someplace pretty important to get to."

Both of the men spoke in the hushed tones of a sick room. The baby whimpered.

Caleb glanced up in time to see Henry clutch the bundle to his chest. "We're not going to hurt you or your mother, son. You know that."

"You want I should go get the buggy?" Doc asked directly in Caleb's ear.

"No, since the horse is bridled, why don't you mount up? I'll hand her up to you and I think Henry here can ride behind. I'll carry Angel."

"Angel?"

"Well, she was born on Christmas Eve and all. I thought

it fittin'." When Doc didn't answer, Caleb added. "She said I could name the baby since I helped birth it." How come he sounded so defensive? Caleb shook his head. "Let's get a move on, okay?"

Doc answered with a snort and, getting to his feet, threw the saddle over the horse's back and cinched it in place. By the time he was mounted and the woman secured in his arms, both men were puffing. Even though she didn't look bigger than a minute, as dead weight she was as cumbersome as a sack of grain.

"Come on now, son. You get up behind here."

Henry shrank farther into the corner, if that were possible.

"Henry." At the sharp command, the boy disappeared into the wood.

Caleb rolled his eyes heavenward. Would nothing go right this day?

He sank down on his haunches, one hand on the manger side. "Now, son." He softened his voice and moved with the slow patience he used when stalking game. "We're trying to take good care of you and your mother. I won't hurt you but you have to mind me. Now give Angel to me and I'll give you a boost up behind Doc Harmon."

Henry wrapped one arm around the now sitting dog.

"Okay, Sam can go with you."

"Caleb." Doc Harmon groaned.

Too late, Caleb remembered Mrs. Harmon didn't cotton to critters in her house. Oh well, what else? He leaned forward and gently unlocked the grip the boy had on the baby. When she whimpered again, Henry started to draw back but after a sigh that came clear from his boots, he scrambled out into the open.

"Now, I'm going to put you up on the horse behind Doc here. Can you hang on by yourself?" Henry nodded.

The saying was easier than the doing. With the bundled baby in one arm, he picked up Henry with the other and hoisted him up. At that moment Angel let out a yell that made her mother moan and raise her head.

"Where? What?" She started to push away. "My baby?"

"You shoulda thought more of her when you started this hare-brained scheme," Caleb muttered.

"Hush, now." Doc spoke firmly using his practiced doctor voice. He explained what they were doing as Caleb took the reins and led the horse over to the door. With a mighty shove, he pushed it open wide enough for the loaded animal to make its way through and turned and closed it when the horse snorted at the wind that had kicked up while they sojourned in the barn. The gray-bellied clouds hung low again, ready to dump another stormy helping.

By the time they reached the doctor's house, snowflakes no longer drifted down but slanted on the wind. Ice crystals from the earlier storm blew off the drifts and stung Caleb's face. He had known a second storm would follow on the heels of the first. Something in his bones told him.

Caleb and the doctor looked at each other, their burdens and back to each other.

"I'll. . ." "You. . ." They spoke at once.

Caleb shook his head and, dropping the horse's reins with the hope the animal knew about ground tying, strode up the snow-covered walk and knocked on the door. When Mrs. Harmon answered it, he handed her the baby with a quick explanation and spun back to get the others. He swung Henry to the ground and reached back up for his mother.

"I'm sorry to be such a burden," Mrs. Carlson whispered when Caleb lifted her down.

"You ain't no burden at all." Caleb hefted her up in both arms, chest high and tight against him. He followed his former footsteps to the open door and, swinging sideways to keep from bumping her, made his way down the hall beside a twittering Mrs. Harmon.

"I'll explain it all later, Martha," Doc growled. "Let's just get her to bed quick as possible. You get some of that willow bark tea seeping and this young pup here might like a cookie."

Sam's toenails clicked on the wooden floor behind them.

"Caleb Stensrude, you get that dog outta my house. You know I. . ."

"Leave it be, Martha." The doctor's tone brooked no argument. He set the boy down and immediately Sam glued himself to Henry's leg. Tail sweeping the floor, Sam reached up to swipe Henry's cheek, once and then again for good measure.

Henry appeared to be trying to fade into the dog's hide. He kept his gaze down so the adults could only see the top of his head.

"Where do you want me to put her?" Caleb called from the hallway.

"Oh, my goodness, in the front bedroom." Martha clucked her way down the hall.

Doc Harmon stooped down and lifted Henry's chin with one finger. "Not to worry, son. Your ma will be all right and Mrs. Harmon just don't like dogs too much. She likes little boys just fine and she'll get used to Sam here." He laid one hand on the boy's shoulder and the other on the dog's head. "You two go on back to the kitchen and wait there. You might take off your wraps and leave them here on the chair."

Like a mouse trapped in a feed barrel, Henry's gaze darted up and down the hall, up to the doctor's face and down to the dog's.

Doc Harmon waited.

As if of their own accord, Henry's hands pulled off one mitten and then the other. When they dangled on their crocheted cord, the fingers eased one button out of the hole and then the other. All the time Henry kept his gaze on Doc Harmon.

"There now. I'm going back to take care of your mother. You two will be right fine here." He paused, gave the boy's head a pat, and headed down the hall.

Mrs. Carlson, now divested of her outer garments, lay under the patchwork quilt in the four poster bed. Her fingers clutched the edge of the quilt as if a windstorm might steal it from her. Her eyes, fever-bright and frantic, appeared huge in her wan face.

"Where's my baby?" Her whisper carried to the man standing with his back to the room, looking out the window.

"Mrs. Harmon has her."

"Caleb, why don't you go see about that poor horse?" Doc entered the room and crossed immediately to his patient. He dug his stethoscope out of his vest pocket and warmed the metal end in the palm of his hand.

"I'm going to take it home and put it up in the barn." Caleb pulled a gold watch out of his pocket. "Then I intend to go join in the Christmas service at church."

"It's almost half over." Doc looked at his friend over the edge of his glasses.

"Not if Reverend Moen tries to make up for no sermon last night." Caleb paused at the door. "Good day to you, ma'am. I surely do hope you feel better soon." He made his way to the kitchen where he could hear Mrs. Harmon talking to Henry.

"Will he be all right here?"

"Landsakes, a'course he will." She set a plate of molasses cookies next to the glass of milk that was already half gone.

A white mustache edged Henry's upper lip. He reached for one of the sugar-topped treats and nibbled on the edge. One hand never left the dog's ruff.

"And the dog?"

Mrs. Harmon looked from the dog up to the quivering boy and back to the dog. Sam wagged his tail and leaned closer to the child, as if he understood he was on trial. "Oh, pshaw, of course he can stay. I'll fix him a nice bed out on the back porch and. . ."

The boy flinched as if she had just struck him. A tear started at the corner of his eye.

Mrs. Harmon threw her hands in the air. "All right, he can sleep by the bed."

A sigh of relief escaped from around another bite of cookie.

"That'll be all then." Caleb crossed the linoleum-covered floor to stand by the breakfast nook. "I will be back later this afternoon. You mind Mrs. Harmon and remember to let Sam out for a run when he asks." The boy nodded.

"You want to come for supper, Sheriff?" Mrs. Harmon asked as he turned to leave.

"Thank you, but I've been invited to Gudrun's. I'll check back though, like I said."

The horse stood where they'd left it, snow clinging to its sorry hide and dusting the saddle. "Poor beast." Caleb brushed the snow off the saddle seat and, gathering the reins, swung aboard. He neck-reined in a circle and started back up the street at a trot.

But Caleb's thoughts were not so measured. What could have frightened her so much she chose to run—in the face of a blizzard—instead of stay where she and her family were warm and dry?

five

Who was the woman with the baby? Who was the dead man they'd found by the livery?

As the choir broke into "Angels We Have Heard on High," Caleb was jerked back to the present. He joined in the hymn but even when he was mouthing the words, his mind remained back at Doc's house. While he hadn't planned on entertaining strangers on Christmas Eve, it had happened. Caleb was of the school of thought that nothing happened without a reason. An angel had come into his life. He knew that for sure, he'd named her. But what about that angel's mother?

He swallowed a gasp. What if she were running from the law? She'd been in such an all-fired hurry to get going again.

When Reverend Moen smiled across his congregation from the pulpit, Caleb had to smile back. Wait 'til the pastor heard about these goings-on, if he hadn't already. The sheriff had worked hand in glove with the Lutheran pastor to help some unfortunates, usually without anyone outside being the wiser, in spite of Mrs. Jacobson and her nose for gossip.

The reverend had reminded his congregation of the perils of that deadly sin more than once but it hadn't seemed to make a difference to certain members of the community.

Caleb looked down the row to the woman in question. Her nose could ferret out the wispiest rumor and she always managed to put her own twist on it before passing the morsel on. She sang on, looking the good Christian praising her Lord on this most holy of days.

"Rejoice for the Savior has come." Reverend Moen could always be counted on for a real uplifting sermon. "Christ is born, and through Him we are reborn every day." As the sermon continued, Caleb tried to keep his mind on the pastor's words. Every time it floated on over to Doc Harmon's house, Caleb jerked it back. He heard phrases like "entertained angels unawares." That sent him thinking about the baby he helped bring into the world. No matter what happened with Mrs. Carlson, he would never regret helping Angel take her first breath. That tiny body that fit into his hands had such a strong pair of lungs, he was amazed. He could feel a smile coming on just at the thought of her.

"Jesus came to bring us love. He is love."

Love all right. He'd felt it burst like a firecracker in his heart when she kicked her tiny feet and flailed those minute hands. Tiny fingers that still managed to wrap themselves around his. Each part of her so perfectly formed. Had Mary felt like this when she held God's Son for the first time? And what about Joseph? Did he have doubts since he knew the baby in Mary's arms wasn't his?

"And now, the blessings of the Almighty God be on and with you all."

Caleb came back to the hard wooden pew with a start. He rose with the rest of the congregation and bowed his head. While the pastor prayed, Caleb added his own. *Please keep them safe and bring health to the mother. Help Doc help her. And thank You for sending them to my house on Christmas Eve. I'll never forget it.* He added his "Amen" to that of the others.

Caleb greeted his friends and neighbors, trying to make his way toward Gudrun without seeming to have any goal in mind. Everyone commented on the blizzard and how abruptly it struck.

"Snuck up on us like a hunting cat," one man said. "And then screamed like a banshee. I told my missus right then there wouldn't be no Christmas program. You shoulda heard my young'uns. Moaned worse 'an the wind."

"Heard there was some poor cuss who didn't make it through the night," someone said. "You figured out who he is yet?"

Caleb shook his head. The speed of the community grapevine always caught him by surprise. "Anyone heard of someone missing? All I know, he ain't from around here." At their headshakes, he excused himself and caught up with Gudrun and Dag Weinlander and his wife Clara at the door. After the usual greetings, he took Gudrun's hand and tucked it under his arm.

"Just to make sure you don't slip on the ice out here." He smiled down at the fashionably dressed woman beside him. A black felt hat with a curled brim and jaunty red feather hid much of her silver hair worn in its usual bun at the nape of her neck. The mink collar of the black wool coat fit snug up to her ear lobes where pearl earrings nestled. With one gloved hand, she grasped the collar more closely to her slender neck. She straightened shoulders already ramrod stiff and returned stare for stare out of faded blue eyes.

"You're looking well today."

"Now, Caleb, you know sweet talking won't cut the ice with me, but thank you, anyway. What is it that's on your mind?"

"Can't I just be neighborly?"

She raised one eyebrow. "Mrs. Olson baked cinnamon rolls this morning."

Caleb sighed. "After all the other things she's been baking? That woman is a treasure."

"So you'll come for coffee?"

"As if I needed a bribe."

Dag Weinlander, owner of the livery and the blacksmith, stopped at her other side. After the greetings, he continued, "Glad you'll be joining us. I hear we have a bit of news to discuss."

Keeping a noncommittal look on his face took effort. Why had he immediately thought of Mrs. Carlson? Surely Dag was referring to the dead man. Caleb just nodded. "I will see you shortly then." He handed Gudrun up into the carriage, tipped his broad-brimmed hat, and headed back up the steps of the church.

The crowd had cleared out faster than normal and there was only one person left talking with Reverend Moen. Caleb waited until the woman moved on, then stepped forward to shake the minister's hand. "Good sermon, Reverend, as usual."

"Thank you, Sheriff." The twinkle in the man's eyes acknowledged his use of titles. "So, how can I help you?"

Caleb checked around to make sure no one else was in earshot. Even at that, he led the pastor back inside the vestibule. "Get you out of that wind." He took in a deep breath. "I have the most amazing story. You talk about entertaining angels. Well, I got me one last night."

At the interest on Moen's face, Caleb told his story. "I'm going to ask Gudrun if they have a place for her, the little family I mean. You s'pose in that big house they have room for a brand-new baby and a little boy who doesn't talk much? Fact is, I haven't heard him say a word so far. And the mother? I think she's mighty afraid of something." Caleb rubbed his nose and cleared his throat. For a man of few words, he'd kinda been runnin' off at the mouth lately.

Pastor Moen appeared to be giving the matter some

thought. He nodded slowly, his eyes glued on Caleb's. "Who else knows about your visitors?"

"Well, Elmer noticed 'em when he came to tell me about the dead body."

Moen flinched.

"I know, I know. But he kinda caught me by surprise. And the baby, Angel, chose that moment to make her presence known."

"Angel?"

"Well, Mrs. Carlson said I could name her and I thought that was about the most perfect name, considering the circumstances and all."

"So what is it you want me to do?"

"Nothing much, I guess. Just wanted you to know the truth of it all, right from the beginning. And people seem to tell you things, so if you hear something I might need to know you could kind of pass it on."

"You want me to go to Gudrun's with you?"

"You want some of those cinnamon rolls too?"

"Mrs. Olson baked cinnamon rolls on top of all the other?" The reverend shook his head. "That woman is indeed a wonder." He paused. "So, are your visitors all right at your house for a while yet?"

Caleb shook his head. "I didn't finish my story. She tried to take off this morning and I found her in a heap in my barn. Doc was with me and we took her directly to his house. She was burning up with fever."

Moen groaned.

"I know, I shoulda got the doctor last night but that blizzard was so bad, I just didn't dare chance it. And now if she. . ."

Reverend Moen held up a hand, along with an emphatic shake of his head. "No, don't you start in again, Caleb. There was nothing more you could have done for your wife and family those years ago and I know you did the best you could here and now. How many times do I have to tell you that Jesus came so you wouldn't have to carry that burden of guilt around any longer? And you don't need to add to it, neither. You hear me?"

Caleb kept his feet from shuffling through an act of will. He knew the pastor was right but the knowing and the doing weren't always the same. He didn't want to count the times they'd had this discussion. Most of the time he was able to agree with the pastor but then something happened like today and he fell back right back in the same old pit. Pastor Moen had worked mighty hard to pull him out of it back those five years ago.

"I'll let you get on to home then, I know your missus is waiting." Caleb reached out and shook Moen's hand. "Merry Christmas. And thank you."

"Merry Christmas, Caleb, and you let me know what happens."

"I will."

After a brisk walk back to his house, Caleb saddled his horse and headed toward Main Street. All the while his hands did as required, his mind gnawed at the twin bones he'd been given in the last twenty-four hours. Two strangers in his town, one bringing death, the other life. Two mysteries to solve. Sheriff Stensrude had never liked loose ends.

Something made him turn down the street to Doc Harmon's before seeing Gudrun.

After a brief greeting, Doc looked up at his guest and shook his head. "I'm afraid it's milk fever, Caleb, much as I hate to tell you."

six

The dead man couldn't be her husband, could it?

Johanna Carlson took a deep breath to still her pounding heart. The baby in her arms squirmed, making the mother realize she'd clenched the newborn to her chest in a ferocious grip. Immediately she relaxed and set the rocker into motion.

She made herself smile at the boy staring up at her, terror rounding his eyes to saucer size.

She had to remind herself that even if this son of hers didn't speak, she could read his reactions better than anyone. He didn't need someone to draw him a map when he could hear what the deputy said as well as she. No child should have to live with more fear in his belly than bread. Hers had for far too long, and it looked to be continuing.

She listened closely to the sheriff's conversation, even though he had dropped his voice. When he turned and asked, or rather ordered, her to stay, she nodded. What else could she do? Only with an effort did she keep from squirming at the discomfort of sitting in the chair. How could she possibly ride the horse after just birthing Angel? And where would they go?

"You just take it easy now," Caleb had turned to her and said. "I'll be back as soon as I can, shouldn't be long."

She nodded, more to say she heard him than that she agreed. How far back down the road do you suppose the wagon is? Is it buried in the snow, not to be found until the spring thaw? If only she had started earlier in the season.

But she hadn't dared.

The dead man—who was he?

The thought that it might be—she couldn't even say his name—Henry's father caused her to grip the rocker furiously with one hand until the room stopped spinning.

"Come, Henry, get your things together. We must be on our way."

The boy wrapped both arms around Sam's neck, all the longing in the world evident in the gesture.

"Henry, son, I'm sorry but you'll have to leave Sam behind. When we get to our new home, we will have a dog again. One that belongs just to you." Memories of another dog put a catch in her voice. "Come now. Mabel is waiting for us out in the barn. Sheriff Stensrude took good care of our horse last night, just like he took such good care of us." She glanced down at the baby sleeping in her arms. "Such good care."

She wished she could unbutton the bodice of her dress, it was so hot in the room. Perhaps she had lost more blood last night than she thought, she felt so weak. And hot. She wiped a hand across her forehead and rubbed her eyes with her fingers. Maybe a glass of water would help.

Carrying the baby in one arm and using the other to brace herself on the backs of the chairs arranged around the kitchen table, she carefully made her way to the sink and dipped water out of the bucket. After drinking, she wet a cloth that lay on the edge of the dry sink and wiped her forehead. She didn't remember feeling so weak after Henry was born. In fact, she'd gotten up and made supper.

She stared across the room to the coat rack by the front door. It seemed better than a mile across the linoleum-covered floor.

"Henry, can you be a big boy and bring Mama her coat?

If you pull a chair over there, you can get both mine and yours down."

Henry buried his face in the dog's ruff.

"Henry!" Much as she hated to, she put a strong dollop of sternness into her voice.

Henry leaped to his feet, eyes wide again and searching the room as if for a place to hide. Sam followed suit, hackles raised, trying to see what was bothering the child.

"Henry, you needn't be afraid, but I need your help. Get our coats now, like a good boy."

Henry shot her a look full of hurt and hustled to do her bidding. By the time he'd retrieved the coats, scarves, mittens, and finally their boots, his lower lip quivered and a fat tear threatened to spill over and run down his pale cheek.

"That's my good son," she said with a smile. Since when did smiling and helping her boy take so much energy? She helped him with one hand, then finally put the baby down on the table to have two hands to dress both herself and Henry. When they were bundled up, she wrapped the quilt snugly around the sleeping infant and, one step at a time, made their way to the back door. Sam acted as if he were tied to Henry's side with baling twine.

Shutting the door firmly on the dog took all her strength. She leaned against the isinglass door to catch her breath. The sun had turned the backyard into a patch of diamonds. Squinting against the fierce beauty of it all through her tears, she followed the trail through the snow to the gable-roofed barn. With each step the barn seemed farther away.

She had to lean against the wooden corner to catch her breath and let some strength return to her knees. Henry sniffed beside her. She looked down to see the tears frozen on his eyelashes.

She looked longingly back at the house. Why had she

left there anyway? Was she out of her mind? The accusations rang in her brain as she struggled to shove open the heavy barn door. She rocked it back and forth, biting back the tears that threatened to run down her cheeks.

Hurry! Hurry! He won't let you go if he comes back. The door finally gave and opened with a shriek of metal on ice. She clung to it as she struggled to get her breath back. "Go on, Henry, get inside where it is warmer." She could hear Sam barking from in the house, so many leagues behind them. Blinking to focus her eyes in the dimness, she ordered her trembling legs to go forward. Spots continued to dance before her. She shook her head, then caught hold of the upright post when a wave of dizziness made her stagger.

Why didn't you stay in the house? Think, woman, think. Like voices in an argument, the words rang in her head. She tried to reason it out. If the dead man were her husband, then he wouldn't be after them. If he weren't, he didn't matter. But then, Raymond might still be on their trail. They had to get away!

"You sit in the hay and hold on to Angel while I bridle the horse." She tried to smile reassuringly but the look on Henry's face told her how miserably she had failed. "Henry, son, you have to help me. Now sit there." She motioned to a mound of hay by the horse's stall. When he did, she laid the quilt-wrapped bundle in his arms. "Just hold her and you'll both be warmer." The words came slowly, in sympathy with her trembling actions.

She looked around the barn and spied a shabby saddle on braces on the wall, beside the one the sheriff obviously used. Without the baby, walking was easier. How could it be so hot in the barn? Was she running a fever? So far to the saddle. She tried lifting it. And tried again. With a mighty heave, she jerked it loose and fell with it to the floor. A wrenching deep inside and a telltale gush told her she was in trouble.

Staggering to her feet, she dragged the saddle to the stall, grabbed the bridle off the nail, and stumbled into the horse's stall.

"Easy, easy." The words came between pants. She leaned against the warm body, trying to absorb what strength she could. When she could stand upright, she stared at the horse's back. She'd forgotten a blanket. Turning, she looked at the saddle blanket covering the other saddle. So far away. Too far. They'd have to do without. She reached down to grab the saddle. The world went black as she collapsed across the leather gear.

seven

"She's going to live. . .isn't she?" Caleb heard his voice break. What was the matter with him? After all, as sheriff he'd seen all manner of life and death. He hardly knew this woman.

But the other side of him, the heart side, chided him gently. *No one could go through a birthing with a woman like you did and not care about her. Maybe there is more to this than you know.*

Caleb ignored that soft prompting as he had the other. "I mean, she has two small children to take care of. They need her."

"Now, Caleb, you think I don't know that?" Doc Harmon rubbed the top of his bald head. "But helping her live at this point is more in the good Lord's department than mine. I'll do what I can and the best you can do is get down on your knees and pray." He picked up the woman's wrist and counted her pulse. "We do the best we can and then leave it in God's hands. That's all."

The sheriff winced. He'd rather go break up a fight in the saloon.

"You'll keep me posted?"

"Of course. You going over to Gudrun's?"

Caleb nodded. "They'll have an idea what to do for her, and the young'uns."

"Ask her if she knows any of the women with extra breast milk. We need to keep that Angel girl alive 'til her mother gets better. Shame I haven't delivered any babies for some time."

Comforted that the doc spoke in terms of Mrs. Carlson getting better, Caleb left him to his ministrations and walked back to the kitchen. Mrs. Harmon had Henry sitting on her lap, albeit a mite stiffly. Sam sat as close to her knee as possible.

"I'll be back later."

Henry's eyes filled with tears. He squirmed to get down.

"No, you stay there. Sam'll be right with you. I need to talk to a friend of mine and then I'll be back. Your mother is in the bedroom back there if'n you want to go see her." He shifted his gaze to Mrs. Harmon. "How's the little one?"

"Sound asleep, the little lamb." The soft and fluffy woman shook her head. "But when she wakes, we better have something here to feed her. Her tummy needs mother's milk, not cow's milk."

"Uh-huh." The sheriff could feel a burning about his ears. All this talk about milk and such, you'd think he'd never had a child of his own. He clapped the Stetson on his head and departed by the front door. Right into another driving blizzard. "Weather 'tain't fit for man nor beast. Leastways, this one ain't as bad as the first." He swung aboard the horse waiting by the gate. As far as horseflesh went, this one lacked some. He dug his heels into the bony ribs and the horse struck off at a teeth-cracking trot until it had to slog through a drift. When it stopped in the middle, the sheriff groaned and dismounted. Muttering all the while, he plowed his way to the front of the horse and broke the trail.

"Come on, horse, pick up your feet."

By the time he reached the big house with gingerbread trim now hidden behind whirling snow, he wasn't sure who was more tired, him or the horse.

He tied the animal inside the carriage house and followed the path that had been shoveled once this day up to the back door of the mansion.

"Landsakes, Sheriff, I thought sure you gave up like any sane man would on a day like this." Mrs. Olson, queen of the kitchen and confidante of the aging Mrs. Norgaard, brushed a trailing tendril back into the bun that seemed to loosen even more. Her always rosy cheeks bloomed brighter from the heat of the stove. "Come in, come in." When he stopped to kick snow off his boots, she took his arm and pulled him past the door to the back porch. "If there ain't been snow on my floor before today, I'd be after ye but right now get over here by the fire and warm yourself. I'll tell herself that you're here."

"What's all the commotion?" Dag Weinlander strode into the room, hand outstretched. "Caleb, good to see you again." He was a man who made most men feel short, but Dag's heart outreached his handshake. Hair the color of summer mink lay close to his head and framed his square jaw with a rich, well-trimmed brush. His blue eyes crinkled at the edges in lines familiar with laughter.

Caleb knew that laughter had not always been Dag's wont. Clara, his wife and a fairly recent import from Norway, made certain he experienced the joys he'd so long done without. "I need to talk with Gudrun and Mrs. Olson, no secrets against you or nothing."

"Well, since this is Christmas and a time for surprises, I'll let you get by with such, this time." He clapped a hand on Caleb's shoulder, pointed to the coffeepot Mrs. Olson had set at the table, and left. "I'll find my womenfolk," he said over his shoulder.

"Now there's a happy man." Mrs. Olson nodded and finished pouring the coffee. "You start with this and I'll get the cinnamon rolls out. I know that's what you really come for." She bustled about the room, setting things out on a tray and glancing over her shoulder, question marks all over her face.

"It's not a secret," he finally said, the cup warming his

hands. "Just thought I'd only have to say it once."

"Have anything to do with that woman birthing her baby at your house last night?"

"Now how did. . . ?" Caleb shook his head. "I mighta knowed you'd a heard already. Ain't nothing in this town sacred?"

"Come on in." Dag motioned from the door. "They're waiting for you."

Caleb picked up the coffee-laden tray and followed his host, leaving a spluttering Mrs. Olson to bring up the rear.

As soon as they were all served to Mrs. Olson's satisfaction, Mrs. Norgaard, in her usual manner, drove right to the point. "You're here about that woman and babe, correct?"

Caleb nodded, still amazed at the efficiency of the town grapevine even in the midst of a snowstorm. He told them the entire story from Sam's first bark. "She's mighty sick and Doc says she may get worse before she gets better." He forced himself to sit still on the horsehair sofa. "I promised the boy his mother would get better, didn't know what else to do." The boy's eyes still haunted him.

"Doc believes she will pull through then?" Gudrun sat in her normal position, back ramrod straight, not even the buttons of her dress touching the back of the chair. Black pointed-toe slippers peeked from the hem of the matching watered silk dress.

"I—he. . ." Caleb sucked in a deep breath. Leave it to Gudrun to cut right to the heart of the matter. "He didn't say that."

"I see."

"What about the children?" Clara Weinlander asked after passing the china plate stacked with cinnamon rolls. Dag took one and passed the plate to Caleb. When the sheriff shook his head, Dag proferred the plate again.

Caleb smiled his thanks and bit into the still warm pastry.

Mrs. Olson could open a bake shop of her own and he would be her first customer—every morning. He finally looked up at the younger woman. "That's a good question." Should he tell them his suspicion that Mrs. Johanna Carlson was running from something—or someone?

"You might as well tell me the whole story."

How could such a dimunitive and elderly woman make him feel as if he'd just got caught with his hand in the cookie jar? And with such few words too. He should take lessons from her. He shook his head. "I wish I knew the whole story. There's been no mention of a mister and none to say she's a widow. To be honest, we ain't had much time for talking, we was busy with other things if you get my drift."

"The children, Caleb, who will feed that baby if her mother has milk fever?" Clara leaned forward.

"I don't rightly know. Doc, he was hoping you'd a heard of someone. Not everyone calls the doctor."

"You could bring the children here, we have room for a wet nurse. Surely there is a woman who would like to earn some extra money."

"Well, now, far as I know, there ain't no money available."

"Now, Caleb, you know there's always money here for those who really need it," Gudrun stated, looking at him over the tops of her gold-framed glasses.

"'Poor but proud' was no doubt quoted with this woman in mind. I can't see her accepting help gracefully.'"

"Graceful or not, she's in no position to argue. We'll deal with her sensibilities in due time." Gudrun raised the bell on the round table beside her chair. "Mrs. Olson will have rooms ready in an hour or so. We'll expect you back with the children before supper which you will eat with us."

Caleb looked over at Dag for support but the man just smiled and shrugged his massive shoulders. After all, what could one do when Gudrun got on her high horse—but set the spurs to your own mount and do your best to keep up?

As Gudrun decreed, by suppertime all had fallen into place. A young woman from the German community just south of Soldahl and her baby were made comfortable in an upstairs room. Her already merry eyes twinkled even more at the sight of two cradles beside a grand four poster bed. In short order she ensconced her month-old son in one and put Angel, after a long overdue feast, to sleep in the other. Henry, with Sam stuck to his side, hadn't left the kitchen, cowering in the warm alcove behind the black and chrome cook stove. He'd managed to put away a couple of sour cream cookies, making sure that Sam got his share, and a glass of milk. Sam licked away the milk mustache which Mrs. Olson ignored for the time being.

She tisk-tisked her way about, preparing the evening meal. "I sure do hope you like chicken and dumplings. 'Course you prob'ly don't have no room left after them cookies but I reckon Sam there will eat what you don't."

"We don't think he is hard of hearing, you know. He just don't talk," Caleb said softly when he entered the room.

"Oh." She lowered her voice.

Caleb nodded and went to squat in front of the boy's hideout. "Henry, I just checked and your ma is doing about as well as can be expected. You come now with me and we'll join the family in the dining room."

Henry shook his head. Sam whined at the stranglehold around his neck.

"Well, now, I sure do think that would be the polite thing to do and all. Your ma would want you to be polite."

The boy looked from the sheriff to the dog and back.

"Mrs. Norgaard, she don't take to dogs in her dining room, I don't believe. Sam will stay here waiting for you."

The boy's hold tightened. Sam gazed at Caleb with imploring eyes.

"Easy there, son, you're about cutting off his wind." The boy released his hold enough to get a quick lick on the cheek.

"You coming, Caleb?" Dag opened the kitchen door. "Oh." He nodded and tongue firmly in his cheek, left. A minute later, he returned. "Bring the dog."

Caleb rose to his feet. "Come on, Sam."

Sam wriggled and stared after his retreating master. He whined.

Caleb slapped his knee. "Come on, Sam."

Toenails tapped on the linoleum floor. The dog whimpered.

"Henry, you can see Sam wants to come. Why don't you do him a favor and let him mind me?" He waited for what seemed like an hour, especially since he was holding his breath. He released it when the boy shifted to his knees and then rose to his feet. Fist still tangled in the fur of the dog's neck, he stopped at Caleb's side.

Caleb's heart turned over at the fear swimming in the boy's eyes. Someone had hurt this child right bad. If only he could get his hands on the swine, he wouldn't hurt any more children, that was for certain. "Not to worry, son. They like little boys here."

Henry took in a deep breath and let it out in a ragged sigh. When Caleb extended his hand, the boy put his in the sheriff's. In fact, that worthless polecat of a man wouldn't get a chance to hurt anyone else ever again.

Caleb lifted Henry up on the stack of books and a pillow set atop a chair, then took the seat beside the boy. Sam thumped his tail, when Henry looked down at him, and licked the boy's hand. Then he stretched out, muzzle on his paws, enjoying a respite from child care.

"Henry, my name is Mrs. Weinlander and I'll help you with your supper if you need it." She looked up to catch Caleb's gaze when the boy flinched away. She smiled reassuringly at the child. "You just nod when the serving things come by."

Dag asked them all to bow their heads for grace and asked the blessing on the meal, including a petition for the healing of Mrs. Johanna Carlson.

Caleb heard the small sniff from beside him at the mention of the sick woman's name. He added a request of his own for the small family facing such trials.

As each dish made the rounds of the table, Henry looked first to see what Caleb took and then nodded at Clara. She put small servings of chicken and dumplings, green beans cooked with bacon, a sweet pickle, and buttered one of Mrs. Olson's homemade rolls.

Conversation flowed along with the good food as each of the adults cast surreptitious glances at the boy eating so carefully but cleaning up every morsel on his plate. Clara refilled his plate when he looked up at her and then toward the platters and bowls.

His mother taught him good manners, Caleb thought, feeling proud as if he'd had something to do with it. He didn't let on that he'd seen the bits that made their way to the dog on the floor. When Gudrun caught his eye, he knew she'd seen too. With the wisdom of years, and the heart of a woman of God, she said nothing.

"Mrs. Olson, you could come cook for me any day." Caleb wiped his mouth with a napkin and watched Henry do the same.

"You know you're welcome here any time." Gudrun made as if to rise. Caleb leaped to his feet and pulled her chair back. "We will have our coffee in the parlor."

Henry's eyes turned dinner-plate size when he saw the evergreen tree nearly hidden by all the decorations in front of the bay window. He stopped in the arched doorway.

Caleb watched as the child stared up and down the tree and then over to the mantel where fat candles nested in pine boughs and cones, finished off with big red bows at either end. The swags on the windows and the garlands that framed every door also received his full attention. Caleb knew what was going through the child's mind. Until he came to Gudrun's house, he had never seen such magnificence either.

Clara came and knelt in front of the boy. "Would you like to come see the tree with me? I like looking at things up close so I can really see them. I'll even show you my favorite ornament."

Henry looked up at Caleb, his eyes asking for permission.

The sheriff nodded. Henry shifted his free hand from the man to the woman. Sam, of course, was a permanent extension of his other.

Caleb watched as Dag's dimunitive blond wife, her wine-red velvet dress pooling about her, knelt in front of the tree and began taking an ornament at a time off the branches and showing it to the child. If adoration had a face, it was Henry's. That Dag was a lucky man. The thought of eyes like precious gems flashed through his mind. He'd only really seen them once. She'd kept her head bowed or her eyes closed much of the time.

Would he ever see them flash again? *Please Lord, let it be so.*

Later Caleb led Henry to the room prepared for him, with Sam in tow. "Now, you'll be just fine right here. Angel is with her nursemaid right down the hall and this here's the bed your ma will be sleeping in, soon as she gets better. You might want to warm it up for her."

Henry hung back, his eyes taking up most of his face.

"I'll wait here 'til you fall asleep."

The boy sighed and began to unbutton his shirt. Tucked up warm and cozy a few minutes later, he clutched the edge of the blankets until his knuckles turned white.

Caleb leaned against the bedpost and wrapped his hands

around his knee. The boy looked lost in a sea of white sheets and pillows. Much against his better judgment, the man looked down at the dog sitting by his feet and thumped the bed covers. With a leap that hardly touched the bed, Sam wriggled under his charge's arm and flicked his tongue over the pale cheek.

Caleb swallowed the rock that swelled in his throat at the look on Henry's face.

Sam twitched the tip of his feathery tail when Caleb whispered good-bye some time later. Henry never stirred. Caleb stopped off at the room where Angel slept in the cradle. He tiptoed in at the beckoning of the young woman rocking her own child by the window. After a smile at her, he leaned over the cradle. Angel lay on her side, tightly wrapped in her infant blankets. She'd managed to free one walnut-sized fist and it lay beside her baby-red cheek. He touched the tiny fingers and instinctively they clasped his.

Caleb beat a hasty retreat. She sure packed a wallop for such a tiny mite.

Back at Doc Harmon's another picture greeted him, this one, too, flushed but restless. Mrs. Carlson moaned and rolled her head from side to side.

"Man, are you trying to freeze her to death?" Caleb whispered. He shot a look of horror at the half-open window.

"Got to get her cooled down somehow and cold clothes alone weren't working. Now I got some snow packed beside her and with the room cold, she's cooling off. You sit here for a while and just talk to her. Tell her about Henry. We got to make her want to live worse'n the easy way out by dying."

"You don't think she's going to give up, do you?" Caleb ignored the pang that shot through his heart.

"That's your job, keep her wanting to live to see her young'uns. I just do the doctoring and I done all I can."

eight

"Angel needs you."

The wind whistled in the gap of the now barely open window, snow powdering the sill.

The woman stirred, her hands plucking at the sheet covering her.

Caleb wanted to cover her with the quilt but he could still feel the fever when he laid the back of his hand to her forehead. But her color was better and he had to grant Doc the benefit of the doubt. After all, he didn't like anyone telling him how to run his job as sheriff.

"Henry, you'da been right proud of him over there at Gudrun's. He is one brave youngster. Now I know he's scared, the fear shouts from his eyes, but he does what he has to do. He and Angel, they're waiting for you to come to them. I thought that in the morning, if you're up to it, I'd bring Henry over for a quick visit. He's pretty worried about you."

Caleb thought a moment. *Now how do I know that for a fact? The boy never said a word.* Could she hear him? *Dear Lord, You can hear me and I know You are listening. All I see is two babes who need their mother desperatelike. So, please, for mercy's sake, let this woman get back on her feet again.* He heard the clock chiming in another part of the house. Doc said he'd be back to spell him about three.

Caleb removed the cloth from the woman's forehead, wrung it out in the pan of water, and replaced it. If only there were something he could really do. He got to his feet and crossed to the window. Fewer flakes were falling and the wind seemed to have let up some. He stuck his hands in his back pockets and hunched his shoulders in an effort to work out the kinks.

Back in his chair he tried to think of something to say. He'd about used up his store of words for the entire week when he noticed a Bible on the bedstand. Flipping to the Psalms, Caleb began to read. "He that dwelleth in the secret place of the most High shall abide under the shadow of the Almighty. I will say of the Lord, He is my refuge and my fortress: in him will I trust."

When the doctor tiptoed in some time later, he checked his patient and nodded. "I think we might have turned the corner, she's sleeping restful now."

"I'll mosey on home then. Thanks, Doc."

"Thank you, Caleb. Any time you get tired of sheriffing, you can sign on as a nurse."

"Yeah, well, think I'll stick with what I know." He snagged his Stetson off the chair back and, gathering up his sheepskin coat, nodded once again. "'Night."

The moon peeked out from behind a cloud, then hid again. The temperature was dropping, Caleb could tell, even as the snow clouds hurried to the south. Still he left the Carlson horse in the doc's barn and plowed through some new drifts on the walk to his house. After hanging up his coat, he stoked the stove again and made his way to the bedroom. Across the foot of his bed lay the red scarf that had been wrapped so carefully around Henry's throat when the little family arrived in the blizzard.

Caleb picked it up and ran it through his fingers. She'd made this special for her boy, he could tell, each stitch perfect and of the softest wool, dyed red to please a boy's heart. "Dear God, don't let up now. Please keep on with Your healing work," he whispered out loud. The house seemed even emptier than usual without Sam.

Caleb fell asleep wondering about the man found dead by the blacksmith shop. Who was he? Maybe the morning would bring some answers.

ॐ

"She's asking for her babes," Doc said with nary a greeting.

"Thanks be to God," Caleb muttered under his breath as if not quite used to saying such things but needing to do so now. "Should I bring Henry over?"

"Yep, and Angel too. Wrap her up in a quilt. Your horse should be able to manage the drifts, though I wouldn't say the same for the sorry piece of horseflesh you left in my barn."

"I know, that's why it's there. Makes me wonder how long they were on the road. May be there hadn't been money for horse feed. Sure does make one wonder."

"You want to put out a notice on the teletype? Mayhap someone's looking for her."

Caleb rubbed the side of his nose. "I think we'll wait. Sent one out already this morning on that man in the morgue." He hoped Mrs. Carlson would tell him about her history herself, soon as she felt up to it. In the meantime, he'd fetch the children. Shame they couldn't use a carriage but none of the streets had been plowed out yet. He knew Clara and Gudrun would make a visit to the sick woman as soon as they could get through.

After the prescribed greeting at the big house, along with fresh coffee and warmed cinnamon rolls, Clara brought the children to him, already bundled up for the trek across town.

"Thank you, ma'am." Caleb drew the red muffler from his pocket and wrapped it around Henry's neck. "So your ma can recognize you. I think you been eating so much good food here, you grew a foot."

Henry flashed Caleb a look of doubt and ducked his head again. One hand still clutched the fur around Sam's neck.

"How about if I take one and you the other?" Dag entered the warm kitchen, all dressed for the elements. "Won't take me but a minute to saddle my horse."

Clara rocked the bundled baby back and forth. "You're going to bring her back, aren't you?"

"You mean Angel or her mother?"

"Both, if you could." She looked down at the sleeping infant in her arms. "I put a couple of diapers in, just in case. She ate about an hour ago." Clara looked up at the sheriff. "You be careful with her now."

Caleb could feel Henry at his side. Perhaps it was a good thing Dag had offered to help. And to think that woman had tried to leave on a rickety horse with both young'uns and sick to boot. He'd have to have a serious talk with her when she had some strength back.

"I know, Caleb, God does work in mysterious ways, His wonders to perform." Clara swayed in the age-old rhythm of women comforting their babes. Caleb didn't pretend to understand the female of the human species. One thing he knew for certain: If anything happened to these two little ones while in his care, the wrath of Clara and Gudrun united would be worse than anything a mere man could dream up.

He handed the mounted Dag the infant after Clara had seen to the quilt flap being tucked over the baby's head just so. Then he tossed Henry up into the saddle and swung aboard, whistling for Sam who'd gone to sniff a bush or two. Together they trotted down the drive that Dag had already shoveled free of drifts and toward the doctor's house.

"Well, Henry, your ma's been asking about you." Mrs.

Harmon unwrapped the boy and hung his things on the coat tree by the door. "And how is our Angel this morning?"

"Now let's forget all that howdy stuff and just bring them back to their ma while she's still awake." Doc Harmon entered the room in a rush. "I got a woman out to the south of town who's set on having her baby a bit early. Martha, you better prepare that other room, just in case."

Caleb and Dag, their charges in hand, followed the blustering doctor down the walnut-paneled hall.

Henry broke away from Caleb's grip and threw himself against the woman lying, eyes closed, in the bed.

"Ah, Henry." She smoothed his hair with her hand. Her voice quavered, shaking like her hand. "I heard you have been a good boy for these kind people." She looked up, a smile almost making it to her face. "Thank you for bringing them."

Dag freed the infant from the quilt and laid her in her mother's arms. "She has been well fed, in fact the wet nurse we found says she eats like a little pig. She will stay until you are able to care for your daughter yourself."

"Thank you." Mrs. Carlson kissed the baby's brow and snuggled her close. "I—I'm sorry to be so much trouble."

"Landsakes, child," Mrs. Harmon said, bustling into the room immediately after her husband left. "Not every town gets its own personal Christmas Angel. You be more a gift than a trouble."

"I'll repay. . ."

Mrs. Harmon threw her hands in the air. "Talk of payment already. You quit worrying about paying and think about getting better. Now, Henry, I got a cup of cocoa out there with your name on it, along with those cookies you liked so well. Sam near to busted down the back door 'til I let him in. He's waiting for you too." She held out her hand

and, after checking for a reassurance from his mother, the boy placed his in her ample grip.

Caleb could hear Mrs. Harmon's running commentary as they made their way toward the kitchen.

"I'll be back in an hour or so to help you with the return trip." Dag said. "I need to check on things at the shop. Will's been taking care of chores over Christmas and I'm sure no one's come in today to have their horses shod." He nodded to the woman in the bed. "Later, ma'am," and left the room.

Caleb took his place in the chair where he'd spent so many hours the night before.

"You were here before, weren't you?" Her voice seemed stronger but not by much.

"Yes."

"I remember your voice." The baby whimpered and stretched her tiny arms. "I—I can't thank you enough."

"The best thanks you can give me is to do what the doc tells you and don't go trying anything stupid again." He could see her crumpled on the floor in his barn. The thought made his throat tighten.

"I won't."

Why was it he could hear a "for now" at the end of her sentence? Stubborn woman. He knew he'd have to watch her. But then, was watching her such a penalty? He shook his head at the silly thought. If he got this poor woman tucked under Gudrun's wing, she'd be safe enough. And considering the verses he'd read the night before about living in the shadow of the Almighty's wings, this small family had plenty of protection.

She was sleeping when Dag reentered the room and the two men made the return trek to the mansion. Angel was letting them know in no uncertain terms that it was feeding time. Henry almost laughed once at Sam's antics playing snowplow with his nose. All in all, it had been a successful morning.

He repeated the process the next morning, this time to find Mrs. Carlson sitting up in the bed. The smile she bestowed on him for bringing her children flew like an arrow straight to his heart. He'd not known she could smile like that, but he did know he'd do anything within his power to bring that smile to her face again.

"The doctor says I can get out of bed soon as I have the strength."

"Now that's right good news." Caleb took his place in the chair.

"He also said that Mrs. Norgaard is planning on taking us in?" A shadow flickered on her brow. She sighed.

"I know, you hate to be a burden. For such a bitty woman you got a powerful sense of burdening." Caleb leaned forward, elbows on his knees. "If'n that is bothering you so much, I got an ideal way you can pay her back." He raised a hand, palm out. "Now give me a minute before you go spluttering at me. We was to have a Christmas pageant on Christmas Eve. The town had been preparing for weeks but the blizzard wiped it right out. Now Pastor says we will have it on Sunday, New Year's Day. There's only been one real problem all along and that's that we've had no baby Jesus. All the babies born around here were just too big for Mary Moen to handle in the manger and all. Now, if you would be willing for little Angel there to star in her first performance, we would all be mighty grateful. Just didn't seem right having a doll play the part, even though Ingeborg Moen made a right fine rag doll of the appropriate size."

Mrs. Carlson breathed a kiss on the brow of her sleeping infant and raised her sapphire gaze to the sheriff's face.

"We'd be right proud to do that. But I have a favor of you. Please would you make sure I get to the service too. If'n I can't walk well enough, perhaps you could carry me."

Caleb knew what the doctor would say. And it would be in no uncertain terms. He also knew what it cost this woman to ask for help. Besides, he'd carried her before and she was some slimmer now. He nodded. "What Doc Harmon don't know can't hurt him. But know this. If you get sicker because of it, he will have my head."

"Thank you, Sheriff." She smiled again and her eyes drifted closed. "Now if I could only stay awake for more'n a couple of minutes."

"I'll be back later with the carriage to take you to Gudrun's house. She thinks you'll get well faster when you can be with your children. And when Mrs. Norgaard says something, not too many of us argue with her." But when he took Angel back in his arms, he realized the mother hadn't heard a word he said. Her soft, even breathing told more of her improving state than her worries about staying awake—and being beholden.

The move was accomplished with a minimum of fuss with the doctor promising to call on his way back from checking on the other new mother.

Clara returned to the kitchen after looking in again on the small family. "They're all sound asleep, Henry curled up next to his mother and Sam on the rug—for a change."

Mrs. Olson shook her head. "Dogs ain't to be in the house, let alone the bedroom." She rolled her eyes heavenward. "But if it helps that little fellow, I guess we'll all put up with it."

"You try to sound so stern, but we all know you have a cream puff for a heart." Clara helped herself to a cup of coffee. "Any word on where they might have come from?"

Caleb shook his head. "I didn't ask but nothing has come through. It's like they appeared out of nowhere. That man that we found dead, though, his family claims he got shot in a fight at the local saloon over in Drayton and hightailed it before the sheriff come. They'll be over for the body tomorrow."

"Such goings-on." Gudrun thumped her cane for emphasis. "So, what's this I hear about our baby playing the part of baby Jesus?"

"I just thought it might help Johanna, er, Mrs. Carlson. . ." He made the change at the raised eyebrow of the town matriarch. "To feel not quite so beholden." He knew better than to call the woman by her first name but it seemed they'd been friends for a lot longer than four days, after what all they went through together. But since when had she become Johanna in his mind?

"That was good thinking on your part." Gudrun tipped her chin so she looked over the tops of her gold wire glasses. "You'd best be careful, though, Caleb. I wouldn't want you to get hurt in all this."

What was she, a mind reader as well? Could she sense what Caleb was already beginning to feel? Caleb took a sip of his coffee. He knew how to keep a close rein on his feelings. . .After all, he'd been doing that for years.

nine

What am I going to do?

Johanna planted another kiss on the soft fuzz of her baby's head. Never had she felt sheets so fine or slept in such a bed with carved posts at all the corners, until she came to this house. Surely she had died and gone to heaven. But the pain in her chest let her know this was still earth. When oh when would she be able to feed her daughter as she ought?

The doctor reminded her to be patient, that the hardness would disappear in a day or two if they kept up the hot packs and let Angel nurse as long as the mother could tolerate. Thank God for that young woman in the other room who had milk aplenty for both babies. So many things she had to be thankful for! She would spend the rest of her life praising God for His boundless kindness.

A soft knock at the door turned her attention away from her worries. "Come in."

Clara pushed the carved door open and stuck her head around it. "I wondered if you felt up to a bit of company?"

"Oh, yes, of course." Johanna tried to push herself up against the pillows. "We might as well send Angel back for a feeding, she got none from her mother."

"Here, let me take her." Clara bent over and picked up the whimpering child. "Oh, Mrs. Carlson, she is so lovely."

"Can't you please call me Johanna? I would be much obliged if you would."

"Of course, and as you know, I'm Clara." She disappeared into the other room where Johanna heard murmurings as the baby was given back to the wet nurse. Patience, the doctor counseled, patience. But lying here with nothing to do. . . .

Johanna threw back the covers. Lying in bed wasn't natural no matter what the doctor said. "Would you please help me to that chair?" she asked when Clara returned to the sick room.

"Uff da, I had a feeling we wouldn't be able to keep you down much longer." Clara wrapped an arm about Johanna's middle. "Just lean on me."

"Goodness." Johanna sank into the rocking chair and breathed a sigh. "I'm so weak. Why, I got up the day Henry was born and cooked supper that night. Whatever is the matter with me?"

"You've been mighty sick, near as I can tell. Fever always takes some out of a person, let alone birthing a baby." Clara took the opposite chair. "Doc says you should stay in bed."

"Well, the doctor isn't here and if I lie there one more hour, I shall go out of what little mind I have left."

"You could read." At the arched look of her visitor's brow, Clara smiled. "Write letters?"

Johanna dropped her gaze to her hands clasped in her lap. *Oh my, if you only knew.* But she didn't dare share her secret with anyone.

"What is it you like to do?"

"Like to do?" Johanna thought of the breathlessness crossing the room had caused. "I can knit, or mend, or do hand sewing." Her hands fluttered, as if needing an anchor. "I need to be doing something."

"All right. We had hoped you would be content to just rest and get well but if this bothers you so much, I will talk to Gudrun and we will come up with something. In the meantime, are you comfortable? Is there anything I can get you?"

Johanna shook her head. "Please, I don't mean to be ungrateful. You have all been so good to me and mine, strangers that providence dropped into your laps."

"No, I understand, I would be the same." Clara rose to her feet. "How about if I help you back to bed for a while and when I return we can take a turn around the room? And you will eat something to make you stronger." She raised a hand to forestall Johanna's objections. "And, yes, I will find something for you to do."

By Friday Johanna could navigate the upstairs but she hadn't yet tried going down the spiraled staircase. With each dawn she indeed felt stronger. The pile of mending had disappeared under her nimble fingers and she itched to use the treadle sewing machine she found in a room down the hall. Never in her entire life had she had so much time on her hands.

Saturday evening the entire town bundled up and strolled down Main Street to the Lutheran church for the pageant. All the participants arrived an hour early to get into their costumes, except for the stand-in for baby Jesus. She was home being fed in an attempt to help her sleep through the performance.

"Are you sure you are strong enough to go?" Caleb had an arm around Mrs. Carlson's waist as they negotiated the stairs.

"Yes, I am. I wouldn't miss this for the world."

Clara followed behind them, babe in arms. "I should be there now to help my class get ready but I know Ingeborg has everything under control. It's not often one gets to carry the star of the show. Makes me wonder how Mary felt."

"She tucked all the things away in her heart, Scripture says. I'm sure she took them all out many times for rumination later." Mrs. Norgaard took Dag's arm. "To think that at one time, Jesus was no bigger than our little Angel here. Astounding, isn't it?"

Johanna kept a tight hold on Caleb's arm. Walking around upstairs was different from coming down stairs wearing a coat and all. She tried to hide her shakiness with a smile but when Caleb put his arm around her waist again, she knew he could see through her.

"I can carry you, you know." His whisper was meant for her ears alone.

She shook her head. What would the townspeople have to say about something like that?

The church Christmas tree stood in the corner ready to have its candles lit, colorful packages stacked beneath its branches. Silver icicles twinkled in the light from the gas lamps and crocheted crosses shimmered white against the green branches.

Caleb looked down at Henry who had the sheriff's pant leg clenched in one hand. Somehow they'd convinced him that Sam didn't go to church. In the faithful dog's place, Caleb had become the safety blanket to which the boy clung. As soon as they were all seated in the front pew, Clara nodded to Mrs. Moen who peeked out from behind the sheets turned curtains strung across the front of the church.

People continued to file in until every pew and chair was occupied and the walls became props for those left standing. When the organ wheezed to life, a hush fell on the room. The lights were dimmed but for the ones in front. Only a tiny giggle from behind the curtains told of those waiting to begin.

Clara took the sleeping Angel back from her mother and sneaked behind the curtain, to return empty-handed. "They promised to take good care of her," she whispered after she sat back down between Johanna and Dag.

Johanna lifted Henry onto her lap so he could see better.

A man's voice, deep and musical, began reading from the Gospel of Luke. "And it came to pass in those days, that there went out a decree from Caesar Augustus. . . ."

A draft skittered across the floor and up everyone's legs. The congregation turned as one to see a young woman on a donkey, led by a boy with an obviously fake beard. The tap-tap of the donkey's hooves provided a counterpoint to the reading. Part of the curtain pulled back to show the Sunday school chorus, singing a song of Mary and Joseph, their eyes shining.

"And so it was, that, while they were there, the days were accomplished that she should be delivered. And she brought forth her firstborn son. . . ." The curtain opened to young Mary Moen, who played Mary, and Will, the blacksmith apprentice, as Joseph, laying an infant in a rough manger. The cow beside them chewed her cud and two sheep knelt in the straw on the floor.

Johanna blinked back tears. Like the family before her, she'd had her baby in a stranger's house and had been surrounded by love and care. As the story and songs continued, thoughts of home intruded. How was he? Was he after her? She quickly joined in the hymn and closed the door on her memories. Here, for now, she and her children were warm and safe.

At the first sign of whimpering young Mary took the baby in her arms and, laying Angel against her shoulder, patted and rocked the infant like mothers the world over. Joseph knelt beside her. The donkey stomped his hoof and twitched his ear. The white-clad children had donned their angel wings to sing again as the shepherds made their way down the aisle. Finally the wise men joined the tableau, in spite of the star that stuck on its wire and refused to hang over the stable.

Reverend Moen finished his reading, the organ broke into "Silent Night," and everyone rose to sing the carol.

Johanna could feel her voice quivering. Never had she seen such a pageant. Never had the age-old story found such a welcoming heart, never had God's Word been made so real. She looked up to see Henry in Caleb's arms and when she swayed, felt Clara's arm go around her waist. She rested between the two strong bodies as the curtain opened again and the actors took their much deserved bow. Angel, wide awake now, managed to free her arm from the confines of the swaddling wraps and wave as if she knew what part she'd played.

The applause finally dimmed, swelled, and dimmed again. Mary Moen left the stage and brought Angel back to her mother.

"Thank you for letting her be in our pageant. What a good baby she is."

"Thank you." Johanna cuddled her daughter close. She looked up to catch a sheen of what? Tears in Caleb's eyes.

He sniffed once and nodded. "She sure is. Not often a pageant gets an Angel to play the part of baby Jesus." His whisper made those around him chuckle.

Back in her mother's arms, Angel fell fast asleep and slept right through the passing out of the gifts from the base of the Christmas tree. When the child still dressed in a white angel costume, with one wing slightly askew, handed a wrapped package to Henry and another one handed him an orange, the stars in his eyes shone brighter than those twinkling in the heavens.

Sitting on Caleb's lap, he looked first to his mother and then up at the sheriff. At Caleb's nod, Henry slid to the floor and, turning, laid his treasures in Caleb's lap so he could open the box. Carefully he untied the string and folded back the red paper. Inside the box was a pair of red mittens and under that a tablet and two sharpened pencils with an eraser.

The smile on the boy's face nearly split the sheriff's heart in two. So much more he had wanted to put in that box but he knew he dared not since that would be showing favoritism. Sure as shooting, one of the more vocal of the church women would comment and make Mrs. Carlson feel bad.

He'd already figured out that staying on the right side of her pride took some real doing.

On their way out of the church some time later, he took care to let Dag shepherd the two younger women and he, with Henry on one arm, extended the other to Gudrun. He caught the flash of humor in her eyes and the slight nod of commendation. As usual, they were in cahoots to keep the gossip mill on a starvation diet.

"I want to thank you all for such a wonderful evening," Johanna said when they had gathered in the parlor after the children were put to bed. Henry had headed for the kitchen and latched on to Sam as soon as Clara removed his winter gear. In spite of Mrs. Olson's tsking, the dog accompanied the child to bed, along with the tablet that he clutched to his narrow chest.

"You are more than welcome." Gudrun smiled at her guest. "I've never seen a more perfect Jesus in a manger. And can you believe how motherly Mary acted?"

"With all the help she's been to her mother in raising the younger ones, I'm not surprised. She is one capable young woman." Clara looked up from her embroidery hoop.

"She's just a little girl." Dag turned from his study of the fire.

"She's ten years old and tall for her age. Can you believe that we had a Mary playing Mary?" Caleb shook his head. "And an Angel playing the best part of all."

"Do they always use real live animals for the pageant here?" Johanna asked. "I've never seen that done before." Of course how could she tell them, she hadn't seen a pageant in years. Not that she hadn't wanted to, but. . .

"Mostly. It gives the children something to worry about besides their lines. That old cow of Doc's knows the program so well by now, it could tell the kids what to do. One year the sheep got loose and took off around the schoolroom, but that was before we had finished the church. No one who saw that one ever forgot it. Mr. Norgaard, bless his soul, was reading the lesson that year. He could hardly continue he was laughing so hard. Mrs. Adamson, she's long gone to her reward too, never forgave him for such hilarity with the holy Scripture."

"I'm surprised they let the animals come again."

"Took a few years but when the Moens came to Soldahl, Ingeborg kind of insisted. To keep from offending the new pastor, the animals returned to the Christmas pageant." Gudrun shook her head with another chuckle. "Oh, the stories I could tell about Soldahl."

"Well, I better head on home," Caleb said with a sigh. "This has been right nice tonight." He got to his feet. "Good night, all."

Mrs. Carlson stood too. "One thing before you go, Sheriff."

He stopped, waiting for her to continue.

"Is there any chance, I mean, I hate to ask but. . ." She twisted her hands and continued on a rush. "Have you been able to find my wagon yet? I need to get on the road again soon as I can."

Caleb felt his breath go out in a rush. A quick glance around the room told him his feelings were shared. What was driving Johanna Carlson that she would risk her life, again?

ten

"For cryin' out loud, woman. . ."

Johanna flinched as if he'd struck her.

Caleb lowered his voice. "I—I'm sorry for shouting like that. Please, please forgive me." Speaking softly and slowly took all his effort. Why did this woman get under his skin like this? He looked up in time to catch a half-smile on Gudrun's face before she had a chance to banish it. Did she know something he didn't? Well, it wouldn't be the first time, that was for sure.

Johanna lifted her chin and seemed to grow a foot taller in the process. "I'm sorry I asked. I will go look for it myself."

"Now, let's take a moment to think on this," Dag said from his place leaning against the mantel. "Mrs. Carlson, there is no way we will allow you to take that sorry horse of yours and go looking for a wagon all by yourself. You have no more idea where it might be than we do since you got caught in a blizzard."

"I agree," Gudrun added with an emphatic thump of her cane. "Your children come first."

At the sound of Gudrun's voice, the starch went out of Johanna's spine and she dropped her head forward. "I'm sorry, you are right. But I don't want to put you out any further. You have all done so much to care for me and mine . . ." She raised her chin again, to half-mast. "How will I ever repay you?"

"Not by running off, or at least trying to—again." Caleb

tried to snatch back the final word but it sneaked out.

"You are correct, Sheriff, there is no need to belabor the point. But as soon as the roads are passable, I must be on my way. I must." She dropped her gaze again when she felt all eyes on her. *What have I done, will they think me mad? Or worse yet, ungrateful?*

"Well, I'll be getting on then. 'Night all." Caleb started for the door and Dag accompanied him.

"Good night." Johanna looked up to see sympathy swimming in Clara's eyes. "If you'll excuse me, I think I hear Angel beginning to fuss. It must be time for a feeding." Lying wasn't usually her way of dealing with such kindness but she knew if she didn't get out of there, she would break down. And there was no way that would happen. She didn't want these people to have to lie for her, if and when he came.

꙳

"I have a suggestion," Gudrun said the next morning at the breakfast table.

Johanna looked up from buttering Henry's pancakes.

Clara paused in the act of pouring a second cup of coffee.

Mrs. Olson nodded. "I figured you would sleep on it and come up with something."

Gudrun dipped her head in acknowledgment. "Near as I can tell, nothing in our home has a rip or tear remaining. There is no hem not sewn back in or lace neatly stitched back in place. Am I correct?" She looked toward Mrs. Olson first and then Clara.

"We do have the upstairs linen closet yet to go through but those things are so rarely used." Clara looked to Mrs. Olson.

"I went through them myself when you were doing so poorly, they are in fine shape."

"That means you have nothing more to do, here, correct?" She eyed Johanna.

"I feel that way."

"I have an idea your fancy work is as meticulous as your mending."

"I try to make it so."

"Have you ever done altar cloths?"

"No, but I've made tablecloths, runners for buffets and dressers, handkerchiefs. I—I used to make them for the local store to sell. There was a shop in town that catered to those with extra money for the finer things. The things I made all sold right away."

"And you can also be a dressmaker?" Gudrun looked over the tops of her glasses.

"Yes, but I haven't as much experience there. You see, I . . ." She clapped her mouth shut. She'd almost said too much.

Gudrun waited. When nothing further was forthcoming, she cleared her throat. "Let us go back to the altar cloths. I would like to donate a set to the church before I die. This has been a long-time dream of mine, but. . ." She shot a glance at Mrs. Olson. "I am not as adept with a needle as I'd have to be, and Mrs. Olson, bless her heart, just hasn't the time."

Clara covered her mouth with her napkin, then excused herself.

"I—I could do that for you? If you tell what pattern you want and all."

"Now, isn't that a fine idea. I'm sure Clara would love to help you and perhaps the two of you could work in some baby clothes too. I keep praying we will have little ones running around here sometime soon." She raised her cup for Mrs. Olson to refill. "If the word gets out that we have such a treasure here, there will be others coming to the door, asking to hire our seamstress."

"Do you think the local general store would be interested in showing some of my things?" Johanna wished she'd kept her mouth closed. If he came looking for her, he'd recognize her handiwork. But he would never spend the money on the train and, as the sheriff had said, the roads weren't passable yet. She should have a couple of months to work on the altar cloths. Not that she'd really need that long. Besides being precise, she had a quick hand.

"Good. Then I will order the linen fabric, I know we have nothing so fine in town. Should be here in a week or two. In the meantime, I know there is some flannel in the sewing room and plenty of fine cotton for baby dresses. You could start with those. Also we could see what is available at Miss Sharon's."

"Miss Sharon's?"

"She's the local dressmaker. I'd have suggested you talk with her but I know she recently hired a young woman to assist her. Right after Christmas is a slow time for all the shopkeepers."

Johanna sat at the table, wondering if this were what being run over by a train felt like. Had she really agreed to do the altar cloths? And told so much about herself? She looked at the satisfied appearance of Mrs. Norgaard and knew she had.

"I think I will send a message to Mrs. Moen to come talk with us. She might even have a pattern or two we could use. I want to keep this quiet. If the Ladies Aid gets wind of it, they'll want to put it all to vote and it would be two years from now before we could begin." She sipped her coffee. "But then I've been known as eccentric so something like this won't surprise anyone."

Clara came back into the room. "We should go over and measure before we order the fabric, don't you think?" She patted Henry's shoulder. "You want to go with me to do that? It's so bright and shiny out, you'd think summer is nearly here."

Henry looked to his mother first and, at her nod, to the young woman behind his chair. If she hadn't been watching, she'd have missed the brief ducking of his chin.

"Good, maybe we'll make snow angels on the way." She took his hand and headed for the coat rack by the front door. "We'll be back later. I know we need some lace and more embroidery thread so I'll go by the Mercantile."

"And Miss Sharon's?" Gudrun asked.

"Of course. Hurry, Henry, before they find more for us to do."

Within the hour Johanna found herself before the sewing machine, hemming flannel into diaper squares. While she'd never used such a fine machine before, she followed Mrs. Olson's instructions and soon had the treadle flying.

"Dinner is ready," Caleb announced from the doorway.

"Oh! You. . .ow!" Blood welled from where the needle stitched right into her finger.

Caleb crossed the room in three strides. He took her hand in his. "Here, let me see that."

Bright red dotted the white flannel and now dripped into his hand. He covered the wound with his thumb and pressed. "This should stop that."

"You startled me."

She looked up into hazel eyes with gold dots around the iris, eyes filled with concern and something else. She'd heard that the eyes were the windows to one's soul and if that were the case, this man's soul was as fine and strong as the hand holding hers. That soul reached out to her with love and compassion.

Love! She snatched her hand from his and looked wildly around the room, anywhere but at his handsome face. When he stepped back, she leaped to her feet and, fleeing to the other side of the table, began folding the stack of squares she'd hemmed. The space between them gave her a chance to recover her breath.

"Mrs. Olson asked me to tell you that dinner is served."

"I—I'll be right down. Y—you go ahead." She glanced down to see a bloodstain on another diaper. "Oh, no."

"You could let me bind that up for you." She could feel his mellow voice clear to the marrow of her bones. What was the matter with her? This had to stop. What if he felt the same way?

The thought brought a lump to the back of her throat. There was no future for anyone in loving Mrs. Johanna Carlson. There was only heartache and possibly even danger.

eleven

Such eyes she had. Deep, fit to drown in.

"Sheriff, you going to Millie's for dinner?"

Caleb thumped the front legs of his chair back on the floor, along with his booted feet. "How many times have I told you not to sneak up on me like that?"

"I—I thought you heard me. I wasn't being extra quiet or nothing." Elmer slouched, like a dog that had just been kicked. "I thought you'd want to know that a teletype just came in, about some missing woman. Since you been looking for something about that Mrs. Carlson, thought you'd be interested is all." He held out a teletype form.

"Well, why didn't you say so in the first place?" Caleb tried to retrieve his heart from down around his boot tops. He laid the paper carefully in front of him. But as he read, his heart settled back in its proper place. This was about some young woman who'd never had kids, just up and disappeared from her home in Fargo. Caleb breathed a sigh of relief. "Send back that we ain't seen hide nor hair of this person. She probably headed to St. Paul or Chicago."

"Sure, boss. By the way, how's that Angel baby and her mother doing? Sure did look mighty purty up there in that manger. Just think, she hadn't come to town, the pageant wouldn't a been near so special. Why I said. . ."

"The reply, man, just send the reply." The sheriff shook his head. Let Elmer get going, and he wouldn't stop jawing for a week. As the man left the office, Caleb almost wished he'd let him talk on. When he wanted to learn the town gossip, all he had to do was get Elmer talking and act the least bit interested.

He propped his boots back up and let his mind wander again. Only now he had more questions than thoughts. Who was she—Mrs. Johanna Carlson? Was that even her real name? Was she a widow? Or was she on the run? The latter seemed the most plausible. She had that running look about her and she had tried to take off right after having the baby. He should know about running. But it had been a long time since he'd felt the need.

He'd even thought of sending out a teletype of his own but something kept him from it. She'd been careful to reveal nothing of her past and that would possibly have been an invasion of her privacy. He thumped his boots back down, rattled the coal in the stove, threw in a big chunk, and shut the damper down. After shoving his arms into his jacket sleeves, he turned the sign on the door to "Closed" and left the office.

A few minutes later he knocked on the door of the mansion.

"Why, Sheriff, how good to see you." When Mrs. Olson opened the door, the fragrance of cinnamon and apple drifted out. "How'd you know I was baking apple pies?"

"Just a sixth sense, I guess. Sure does smell mighty good. You know if you'd open a place down on Main Street, I wouldn't have to come so far for my coffee."

"Don't you go giving her any ideas, we'd be lost without her," Clara admonished with a wide smile as she descended the curved walnut staircase. "Come with me and we'll fix up a tray. I know Johanna is due for some refreshment too."

"Seems to me we see the sheriff more since she moved here," Mrs. Olson murmured just loud enough to be heard by the two in front of her.

"But we'll never tell, will we?" Clara whispered back.

Caleb could feel his ears heat up like someone held a candle right beside them. "Where's Gudrun?"

"Working on her accounts. She will join us."

Caleb leaned over to sniff the perfume rising from the slits in a golden pie crust. "Ah, if I were the marrying kind, I'd ask you to hitch up with me in a minute." He closed his eyes, the better to savor the fragrance.

"If'n I were twenty years younger, I'd take you up on it." Mrs. Olson swatted his hand away from the knife on the table. "Leave off, I'll make sure you get an extra large piece. Here, I thought this was for after dinner."

"There's plenty for that too. Dag over at the shop?"

"Ja, he don't take off midmorning like some we know."

Clara giggled from pouring coffee into the silver server. "I'd be willing to bet money that he'll show up too." Just then the sound of snow being kicked off boots at the back door made them all laugh.

"Right on time," Caleb called to the man removing his coat on the porch.

"I smell apple pie." Dag hung his coat on the tree by the door. "Something told me I was needed at home." His grin set his blue eyes to twinkling. He crossed to the sink and began scrubbing his hands.

Clara sniffed. "You've been at the forge."

"Ja, that I have. Two teams needed shoeing and Anselm brought in his plowshares at the same time. That is one man that plans ahead. If all the farmers thought like he does, we'd have more steady work and less of a rush at plowing time." He dried his hands just in time to take the tray from his wife and lead the way to the parlor.

Clara flew up the stairs to the sewing room, her voice calling Johanna as she ascended.

Gudrun came out of her study, leaning slightly on her cane.

"I thought I heard a party in the making. Now, where did that Henry take off to?"

Caleb remained at the door to the parlor so he could watch the stairs. Clara came first, Henry's hand in hers. Sam looked down at his master, up at the small boy, and back down as if to say, you told me to take care of him, I'm just doing my job. Caleb nodded his approval and Sam wagged his tail.

"Johanna will be right down, she's just changing the baby."

Good, Caleb thought, *then I get to see Angel too.* He followed the others into the room that now seemed bare without the Christmas tree in the bay window, and took the chair with a view of the stairs. When she came down, the smile she bestowed on the infant in her arms made him catch his breath. Her smile radiated pure love like the sun radiated warmth. The pallor was gone from her face, along with the lines of worry she'd tried to disguise. Instead of the dark skirt and much-worn waister, a gown of green serge, trimmed in black at the collar and cuffs, set her eyes, those incomparable eyes, to sparkling.

He only got a glimpse of that sparkle but it went right to his chest. Would she ever look at him like that? The thought made him choke on his coffee.

"Are you all right, Sheriff?" Even her voice sounded different, more assured, not so tentative.

"I—I'm fine." He swallowed and coughed again. "Just went down the wrong way." He looked up in time to catch a knowing glance shared between Mrs. Olson and Gudrun. Was he so transparent?

Johanna bent over and held Angel out for him to see. "She's started smiling already."

Caleb touched the tiny fist with a gentle finger. Immediately Angel wrapped her fingers around it and turned her head at the sound of his voice.

"Angel, baby Angel, how you doing?" The grasp of her tiny fingers felt like a gift from above.

The tiny, perfectly formed lips twitched and spread in a smile. If he'd delighted in the grasp of her fingers, the smile did him in. She studied him and he her. He touched her cheek with the knuckle of the finger she held and the smile came again.

"She likes you."

"She better. She and me, we had quite a discussion that night she came into the world." He looked up at Johanna. "You don't suppose she remembers me—my voice, do you?"

"Why not? We have no idea how much babies remember. You want to finish your coffee and you can hold her?"

Caleb put his coffee cup back in its saucer on the table beside his chair, beside the plate of pie with only one bite taken. "I'll take her now. You go enjoy your pie."

Angel snuggled into his arms with a big burp. Johanna quickly laid a cloth over Caleb's shoulder and arm. "Just in case."

"Yes, it wouldn't do for our sheriff to patrol the town with baby spit on his shirt." Gudrun lifted her cup to lips that twitched to keep from smiling.

Caleb ignored the chuckles and, in a low voice, kept up a running commentary to the baby in his arms. So long since he'd done this with his own two small ones, he'd have thought he'd forgotten how. But it all came back with a rush. The sweet smell that only came from a baby, the tiny weight of her, the eyes that wouldn't let him go. He knew they said that babies couldn't focus this soon, but he'd bet his badge that Angel was looking right at and through him. She stretched, her arms reaching from the blanket wrapped so tightly around her. Tiny fists waved in the air and she scrunched her face at the same time. She burped again, this time a stream of milk coming out the side of her mouth.

Caleb used the cloth and wiped it away. When Johanna motioned that she'd come get her daughter, he waved her away. "She's fine here."

"But your coffee is getting cold."

"No, never mind." Caleb rocked a bit in the chair. Henry and Sam came to stand beside him. The two might well have been lashed together for the tight fit they were. Henry's hand looked to be permanently embedded in Sam's neck ruff.

"So, you think she's okay? For a three-week-old baby, that is? I know you can't play with her much yet but one day you will." Henry looked up at the sheriff and back at the baby. He leaned slightly against the man's knee, his weight barely felt. As Caleb carried on his one-sided conversation, he continued to rock Angel until her eyelids drifted closed. She yawned, her lips forming a perfect *O*, her eyes wide. After one more relaxing sigh, her eyes jerked open along with her hands and then closed again.

"She's asleep." Caleb whispered and Henry, bless his heart, nodded. Between the two, Caleb felt he'd been given a medal.

"You want me to take her?" Johanna started to rise.

"No, we're fine." He'd transferred one hand to Henry's shoulder and commenced to stroke the boy's back, just as he would a high-strung horse. The boy could hear, he was smart as any ten-year-old if not more, and, wonder of all wonders, he was leaning into the stroking like he couldn't get enough. Quite a fine piece of work for one morning.

Johanna watched the three from across the room. How could she keep them all from becoming too attached? She would be leaving as soon as the weather allowed. Poor

Henry, to be offering his trust only to have it rudely taken away again. But wasn't it better to have love in your life, even if you would lose it again, than to have no love at all?

She sighed. To whose heart was she speaking after all?

"I need to get back to those altar cloths, if they are to be finished this winter." She refolded her napkin and laid it on the tray.

"That gold thread tangles something awful," Clara added. "I'm wondering if there is something we can substitute." She got to her feet along with Johanna. "I follow my slave driver back to work."

"You needn't. . ."

"Johanna, I'm only teasing." She put her cup and saucer on the tray. "Thank you, Mrs. Olson, for your usual delicious delicacies. If you need me, you know where I am."

In a flurry of skirts, the two took the children and headed back up the stairs.

Johanna looked back down once to see Caleb watching her. She started to smile, nodded instead, and continued after Clara. The picture of him with her children refused to leave her mind.

❧

The days fell into a pattern with caring for the children, working on the altar cloths, and visiting with Gudrun, Clara, and Mrs. Olson, who always found ways to entertain Henry. He could usually be found in the kitchen, helping with the baking. She was never sure how much of his dough went into the rolls or cookies and how much went into him. If he weren't kneading dough he might be reading in the library with Clara, or in the study, intent on following the lines Gudrun drew on the paper that became his letters. He could now write his name without coaching.

When company came, which was often, Henry fled

upstairs to play quietly beside his mother.

Johanna enjoyed working with the fine material and lovely threads for the altar cloths. They were doing green, purple, and white for the major liturgical seasons, of which she'd had no inkling until now, attending the Lutheran church with her mentors. The stack of baby things grew too, far more than Angel needed.

Clara wanted a baby. Dag wanted a son. Gudrun wanted children running through the house and even sliding down the banister. But so far, it hadn't happened.

How will I ever repay them for all their kindnesses? The thought ran through Johanna's mind often and with never an answer. She'd never had life so easy. No housecleaning, or at least very little. She insisted on keeping up her own rooms, including the sewing room, but Mrs. Olson and a woman they had come just to clean, kept up the rest of the house. A woman collected the laundry each week and brought the clothes back folded or ironed and ready to put away. All but the diapers, which Johanna insisted on doing, and even for that, she had to struggle to keep ahead of Mrs. Olson.

"Why, I can do a boiler of those while the soup's cooking," she'd say. "You just keep on with those lovely things you're working on. What a surprise that will be to the folks at the church."

But somehow the news got out that there was a new seamstress in town and since Miss Sharon only did dressmaking for women and older girls, soon customers were beating a steady path to the mansion door.

"I can't turn your home into a sewing shop," Johanna said one day in mid-February. She stood before Gudrun's desk in the walnut-paneled office. Walnut file cabinets took up the space between the two tall windows and lawyer's bookshelves with glass fronts lined another wall. Johanna forced herself to stand straight and not squirm. The formal room made her feel like whispering.

"Have I complained about all our visitors?" Gudrun clasped her hands on the green felt blotter.

"No, but. . ."

"But?" Gudrun nodded to the chair in an invitation for Johanna to sit.

"But it just isn't seemly. Yours is such a fine house, better than the likes of I could ever dream of." Johanna sat on the edge of the seat, her back as straight as that of her mentor.

"This is no longer my house, as you well know. I too live here on sufferance and when Dag and Clara are happy with the arrangement, so am I. And so should you be."

"Oh, please, do not think I am not happy. I have never lived in such splendid surroundings and when we leave here, it will be difficult to adjust again. That is part of my concern." Johanna leaned forward. "You know, I cannot stay here forever."

A smile touched the corners of Gudrun's mouth. "Why not? There is plenty of room and you have certainly made yourself useful. I can see you helping Mrs. Olson more as she suffers from the lumbago at times. And I believe I know of a man here in town who will come courting as soon as you give the word."

Johanna could feel the blood leave her face. Suddenly she felt lightheaded. "That can never be." Even she could hear the stark despair in the simple words. She shook her head and studied the recent needle prick on the side of her thumb.

"Johanna, I know there are things from your past you want, you need, to keep to yourself. Once I heard Reverend Moen say that a sorrow shared is cut in half. Let me help you with your burden."

"I can't." Johanna shook her head again, slowly as if it were too heavy to move. "I simply cannot."

twelve

"They're finished." Johanna set the last of the flatirons back on the stove.

Clara traced the cross embroidered in gold thread on the set of white cloths. "I was beginning to wonder if we'd make it before Easter. I know Gudrun hoped to present them in time for the Easter services." She looked over at Johanna. "What a lot of stitches." She raised a much-punctured finger in the air. "And I have the holes to prove it."

Johanna looked at her own hands. She'd taken to putting goose grease on them at night to keep them soft. But her hands this winter were a far cry from usual. Without cows to milk and floors to scrub, her hands had the look and softness of one no longer used to heavy labor. Hardening them up again would take some doing.

"Let's call Gudrun so she can see them before we pack them all up again. I'll put the coffeepot on and you go get her."

"What about Mrs. Olson?"

"She went to the store and then planned to stop and visit with one of the church ladies." She glanced out the window. "I hope she gets back before the snow starts again. I was hoping this was the real thaw and not just a teaser."

"It's too early for that."

"I know, but I want to get out in the garden and bring cut flowers into the house. You should see that front entry when I have a big bouquet of lilacs or roses on the table, reflecting in the mirror. When I was in Norway, I never dreamed of flowers like the ones that grow here. And when I don't have to do all the spading and weeding, it makes them even more pleasurable." She rattled the grate and added several pieces of split wood to the coals. "Wait until you see our garden out in the back. Dag said I could add more roses this year and I'm looking for a yellow one. I love roses, don't you?"

Johanna nodded. The only roses she'd ever had were the wild ones she cut by the road and they never lasted long in the house. Best they be left to grow into hips for making tea in the winter. "I'll go call Gudrun."

How do I tell her I will not be here to see the roses bloom, to smell the lilacs? Perhaps there will be lilacs where I am going? She took in a deep breath and let it all out on a puff. If only she knew where she was going. Probably as far west as the wagon and the horse would go. When they stopped, she would too, and hope to heaven there was a place for her to work or land to homestead. She'd heard there were still sections to homestead in parts of South Dakota or on the western edge of North Dakota.

She tapped on the office door.

"Come in."

Johanna pushed the door open to see Mrs. Norgaard down on the floor on her hands and knees, helping Henry build a tower out of the odd-shaped pieces of wood that Caleb had carefully cut and sanded. When he gave the boy the box, Henry's eyes lit up like the forge in full spate.

"Well, I never."

Gudrun leaned back against the chair and straightened her skirts. "You caught us in the act, didn't she, Henry?" Like everyone, she included Henry in her talking as if he carried on a conversation like all the others.

Henry's smile wreathed his face when he pointed to the

intricate edifice they had constructed, including even the chair leg in their plans.

Johanna knelt down and peered inside. "That is a mighty fine building."

"It is a church. We just ran out of lumber for the steeple, didn't we, son?" Gudrun staggered to her feet with a groan and a dusting of hands. "Been too long since I've been down on the floor for anything." She reached over to give Henry a hand. "Come along, I'm sure you and Sam will be able to put away a cookie or two." The dog wagged his tail from his place in front of the crackling fireplace.

Barely able to contain her laughter, Johanna followed behind the three as they marched out the door. No one outside this family would believe her if she announced Mrs. Norgaard had been building with blocks. But then, she'd never tell. This would be another of the memories she was storing up for the dry spell ahead.

"Wait until you hear the news." Mrs. Olson came through the back door like she'd been blown in by a blizzard. "Oh, my land." Her voice softened when she caught sight of the paraments for the altar spread around her kitchen. "If that ain't the purtiest. Wait 'til the reverend sees this." She fingered the gold fringe tied so carefully on the ends of the pieces. "If that ain't to beat all." Dabbing at a tear that had gathered at the corner of her eye, she looked up to catch Gudrun's smile. "This will do you proud, that's for sure."

Johanna and Clara opened the box they'd been saving for just such a time as this. With tissue paper between each piece, they laid them all in the box, color by color, ending with the purple since that would be used first. When they closed the reinforced carton, Mrs. Olson took a string and tied it around both ways several times.

"Just in case. Be a shame to get anything so fine, dirty,

even by accident." She clasped her hands over her heart. "I know God will be glad to see His house fancied up with these for Easter."

"I think He's more concerned about the state of our hearts, but we won't argue the point." Gudrun took a place at the table. "Now, I heard there were cookies for a starving boy and perhaps even his old friend. What do you say, Henry?"

They were sitting around the table enjoying the cookies and coffee when Mrs. Olson slapped her hands on the table. "Oh, in all the excitement, I forgot to tell you my news. Miss Sharon is getting married and moving to Montana and wants to sell her shop. All I could think was what a perfect place that would be for you, Johanna."

"Me? But I have no money to buy a business." Johanna coughed on a cookie crumb that stuck in her throat. "What an outlandish idea."

"I think it is a fine idea." Gudrun set her cup back down precisely in the groove of the saucer. "I know this must be an answer to our prayers."

"Whose prayers?" Johanna's voice squeaked on the last word.

"Mine and Clara's. And I know you've been praying for help too but you haven't shared what you wish with the rest of us. Johanna, we only want what is best for you, but I must confess my selfishness in wanting you to remain in Soldahl."

"And mine." Mrs. Olson beamed from one to the other. "I just knew this was the most perfect thing. Not that Miss Sharon won't be missed, but you will be able to stay here."

"I don't have any money to buy a business." *Even if I could stay here,* she thought desperately.

"That can be worked out, I'm sure." Gudrun turned back to Mrs. Olson. "Did you find out when she is planning on leaving?"

"Of course. She hopes to be gone by Easter. If she hasn't found a buyer by then, she will just pack it up and take the merchandise with her. She said the bank owns the building anyway, but then I 'spect you know that already."

Gudrun nodded. "The bank holds the note. Ernest Hopstead gave her the loan on my say-so, what, seven years ago, and since then she's renewed the loan to buy more supplies. I hate to see her walk away from her investment like that without recompense."

"Well, she has stars in her eyes for sure. She thought she was long past marrying age and here that drummer just whisked her off her feet. She said he's saved up enough to start a horse and cattle ranch with his brother in Montana."

Johanna listened to the conversation eddying around her. Was this her chance? Had God really heard her prayers and was now answering?

She remembered the night of the blizzard that blew them to Sheriff Stensrude's doorstep. Seemed she'd been praying nonstop since long before the wagon got caught in the drift. And once they mounted that old nag, she'd pounded the gates of heaven for sure. She hadn't dared take a better horse. . . . She stopped the memories before her friends could read anything on her face.

"I would love to be able to stay in Soldahl but I just don't think it is possible." She watched Henry's shoulders slump. *I know, son, if there were only a way.*

Looking up, she caught Gudrun's stare over the tops of her glasses, a look that penetrated to the bone. The desire to tell the truth welled up and could only be capped with a supreme act of determination, the same determination that had kept them on the horse when the wind tried to blow them clear to Texas.

"Well, we will have to discuss this later." Gudrun laid a

hand on Henry's shoulder and smiled down into his upturned face. "Henry, would you be so good as to fetch my shawl? I left it on the back of the chair in my office." When the boy slid from his chair and darted out of the room, she turned back to the others. "I believe this is better discussed without him present. Now, Johanna, I know how happy you are here, it is evident in your face and bearing, besides in the wonderful stitching you do. I believe your owning that business would make a fine addition to the life of Soldahl and you all know that is something near and dear to my heart. If you feel you can remain here, we will work out some kind of terms for you to purchase that business. Miss Sharon has a nice little home in the back of the shop and there is a fenced yard and pasture beyond that."

Henry appeared in the doorway without a shawl.

"Oh, I'm sorry, child, I must have left it on the end of my bed."

Henry darted away again and they could hear Sam's toenails clicking on the newly waxed floor.

"Wouldn't you at least like to go look at it?" Gudrun asked with a gentle smile.

Oh, if you only knew. The thought of having a shop like that of her own was a dream come true. Could it really happen? Was she safe here? Soldahl wasn't really on a road to anywhere. Would he look here? If he were looking. Had God answered another prayer and protected them from his wrath by sending him elsewhere? How long could she go on living this lie? Or was it a lie? She'd never told them she was a widow. *But you let them assume that,* she scolded herself silently. If only that gentle little voice would be quiet.

She drew herself up straight, as if pulling her feet out of mud. "I would indeed like to go look at the shop. If you think it possible for me to make our living there, then it is worth looking into."

"Thanks be to God." Mrs. Olson breathed the prayer on a sigh.

Henry trotted into the room and handed Mrs. Norgaard her shawl of soft rose wool.

"Thank you, dear boy. Here, would you please help me put it on?" With his assistance, the shawl rested around her shoulders and somehow her arm found its way around his waist. He leaned against her, one hand smoothing the softness of the wool.

Johanna sighed. What a bundle of conflicting feelings she had stuffed in her heart. But she knew she'd made a wise decision. Henry needed the love and attention he received from these dear people like the spring soil needed rain and sun. Even if they were forced to flee again, he would always have this time to remember. As would she.

"When do you suppose we could go look at it, the shop, I mean?"

"The weather is somewhat inclement for me today." Gudrun glanced out the window. "But I see no reason why you and Clara could not go. Mrs. Olson and I will keep the children here until you return. Please ask Miss Sharon to make an inventory of the supplies she has in stock and an estimation of what she would like for those materials. I will ask Ernest at the bank what he values the building at and the amount of the loan remaining."

A wail could be heard from the nursery upstairs.

"There is Angel. I will go feed her and then change into something warmer."

"I will be ready by then too." Clara leaped to her feet. "This is so wonderful."

"I will have a couple of notes written for you to deliver."

Gudrun rose to her feet also. "Henry, I do believe Mrs. Olson needs some wood carried in from the porch to her woodbox. What do you think?"

Johanna left the kitchen as Henry hit the door to the porch running. "You better put a coat on," she threw over her shoulder, knowing that Mrs. Olson would never let the boy go outside without one. They all took such good care of him and made him feel important by asking him to help. How blessed they were.

A peaceful quiet filled the nursery as she settled Angel against her. The baby rooted around, making snorting noises that turned to the song of suckling. Her deep blue eyes fastened on those of her mother and a gently curled fist found its way to the curve of her mother's body.

Johanna felt the clutch in her throat that came so often in this moment. The rocking chair creaked its song, with the brush of her foot against the rug as a counterpoint. The creak and swish lulled both her and the babe.

The sound of the front door opening jerked her fully awake. If they were to call on Miss Sharon, she'd best hurry. Rising to her feet, she heard the sound of Caleb's voice teasing Mrs. Olson.

Please don't tell him what we're thinking of doing. The thought caught her by surprise. "Why ever not?" she whispered to Angel as she laid the baby back in her cradle. But deep inside, she knew the answer. Perhaps she could live in Soldahl, but she could never allow her feelings for the sheriff to be known.

thirteen

"Oh, my."

"What is it? Don't you like it?" Clara turned to the woman following her into Miss Sharon's dressmaking shop. A bell over the door announced their arrival.

"Oh, no, I mean, that's not it at all." Pausing at the first shelf of materials, Johanna stroked the bolt of emerald green velvet with just the tip of her finger, as if a firmer caress might make it disappear. Matching laces and ribbons vied for attention beside the velvet; to the right lay bolts of fine wool, both gabardine and worsted. Hat frames hung on pegs along the upper wall, while summer dimities, calicos, and ginghams invited her perusal on another wall. The jewel tones of the silks took her breath away.

"May I help you?" A woman brushed aside the curtain covering the door to what Johanna supposed was the workroom and the living quarters. With light brown hair coiled in a no-nonsense bun, lively brown eyes, and a slightly red nose that twitched mischievously, Miss Sharon reminded one of a friendly field mouse. "Why, Mrs. Weinlander, how nice to see you."

"Thank you, Miss Sharon. I'd like you to meet my friend, Mrs. Carlson."

The mouse twittered. "Oh, you're the mother of the darling baby who played Jesus at the pageant how is she and you I hear you are a wonder with a needle and thread we have so much in common won't you come sit down so we can visit or is there something that you need here in the shop?"

Johanna felt like she needed to gasp for air. Did the woman never stop to breathe? Which of those questions should she answer first?

"Oh, excuse me, I know I get a bit carried away at times. How is it I can help you?"

"We've come to talk with you about your shop." Clara included Johanna with a glance. "Mrs. Olson said you are looking to sell."

Miss Sharon gestured for them to follow her. "That I am, so let's sit where we can talk comfortably, then I will show you around."

Johanna looked at Clara to get a wink in return.

"She takes a bit of getting used to," Clara whispered as she led the way behind the shop owner.

"Uff da." Johanna spoke for Clara's ears alone.

A broad cutting table and a sewing machine proclaimed the room they entered to be the workroom. Miss Sharon beckoned them through another curtained doorway, into a cheery kitchen and parlor all rolled into one. A red and white checked cloth covered the square oak table and matching cushions the seats of the ladder-backed chairs. Curtains of the same bright fabric at the windows made even this gray day bright. Braided rugs on the floor, a tabby cat snoozing in front of the cast-iron stove, and a teakettle whispering on the back burner all said "home" to Johanna.

"I've the teapot hot if you would like to join me for a cup of tea. I've been so busy I haven't taken time for a setdown all day."

"You have new orders then?" Clara took one of the chairs at the table.

"Landsakes, all of a sudden everyone wants new Easter dresses and they didn't say anything until I announced that I was leaving." Miss Sharon bustled about her kitchen,

measuring tea leaves into a china pot and setting out cups.
"I thought to make me a new dress for the wedding but
George, have you met George Drummond, he's my fiancé."
She said the word with obvious delight. "He says he don't
want me to spend more time here than necessary. He's ready
to leave for Montana, the sooner the better. I thought to
having a close-out sale but if I can sell the shop and my
business together, someone else will be all set. I've made a
good living here and the people of Soldahl much appreciate someone knowing style and fine sewing. Even though
Mrs. Jacobson over at the Mercantile carries ready-made
now and you can order from the Sears and Roebuck catalogue, when the women want something special, they come
to me."

"I heard you had to hire a helper." Clara accepted the cup
of tea with a smile. "Thank you, this is such a treat."

"I did, and I was hoping she might take over here but at
the suggestion of that, she ran like a scared rabbit. Guess
she was afraid I was going to head out at night and leave
her with all the work or something." She lifted her cup and
sniffed the aroma. "Nothing like a nice cup of tea on an
afternoon, I always say. Coffee is for morning and tea for
afternoon." She pushed a jar across the table. "Here's honey
if you like a dollop of sweetness."

Johanna sipped her tea, wishing she could be in the other
rooms, going through all the drawers from the smallest that
might hold buttons to the large bins for fabric bolts. She
wanted to touch each bolt of fabric and run her fingers over
the feather boa draped over the dressmaker's form in the
corner.

The bell tinkled out in the shop.

"I'll be right back. Probably someone to pick up their
order." Miss Sharon bounced to her feet and out the door.

"Oh, the look on your face." Clara leaned forward so she

could talk softly.

"Am I so obvious?" Johanna shook her head. "She is amazing."

"That she is and in a hurry to leave for Montana. You could finish all those dresses as well as she can."

Johanna sighed and shook her head. "Clara, I know you have a heart of gold but I cannot afford a place like this, all the lovely materials and such. And the banker here, he doesn't know me from Eve to give me a loan and. . ."

"Just you leave those worries up to Gudrun. She still owns that bank and. . ."

"Gudrun owns the bank?"

"Ja, didn't you know? When her husband died, she kept the controlling ownership and the manager, Mr. Hopstead, owns the rest. She thought that way he would be more inclined to manage it well. Not that he wouldn't anyway, you understand, but he'd been Horace's second in command and it just seemed fitting."

Johanna sank against the back of the chair. "No wonder she knows so much of what goes on around here."

"She knows a lot more than she ever lets on or shares with the rest of us. When someone confides in Gudrun Norgaard, you know your secret is safe with her. Your business will never be discussed over the back fences like some others I know." Clara bobbed her head for emphasis.

"There now, where were we?" Miss Sharon set the curtains to flapping on her way back in.

"I think we would like you to show us around a bit more, there are bedrooms upstairs, is that right?"

"And a bit of a barn out back. I used to keep a horse but finally decided I didn't need one. Everyone comes to me if they need sewing done." She crossed to a door to the back. "Here, I'll show you the pantry first."

Dusk shadowed the land by the time the two women

walked up the street to the Norgaard mansion. A gas lamp outside the front door welcomed them home and the smell of supper cooking greeted their entry. Henry threw himself against his mother's skirts.

"Here, let me take off my coat first." Johanna patted his shoulder and cupped his cheeks in her hands. "What's this I see, I think someone had a cup of cocoa." He tried to lick the evidence off, the tip of his tongue doing its best. Johanna took his hand after hanging up her outer things. "Come, let's go wash you up and then I think I hear Angel crying. Has she been good? Have you?"

He nodded and tugged on her hand. In the kitchen Mrs. Norgaard sat in the rocking chair by the newly blackened stove and held the baby flat on her back resting on her knees between the woman's two arms. Angel appeared to be hanging on every word the old woman whispered and sang.

Johanna stopped in the doorway to better appreciate the scene until Angel tightened her face and whimpered. Her mother knew that whimper would soon turn to a squall if not interrupted quickly. "Here, I will take her. Thank you for watching her."

"So long it has been since these old arms held such a beautiful infant as Angel." Gudrun handed up the baby with a sigh. "It seems like a lifetime ago since my Harold was that size, if he ever were."

Johanna paused. For some reason she'd thought Mrs. Norgaard had never had children.

"Yes, he died of the influenza the year he was three and the good Lord never saw fit to bless us with another." A shadow hovered in her faded blue eyes. "I still sometimes wonder why."

"That's so's you'd have time for all the other children you've helped and the families who bless you every night for one good thing or another. You treat the whole town of

Soldahl as your family—and half the countryside." Mrs. Olson leaned over to check the chicken she had roasting in the oven. Her face flamed red from the heat of the open door.

"Ja, that is true." Clara joined them, a sheaf of papers in one hand. "Here are the papers you wanted from Miss Sharon. She said she knew a buyer would want them so she had them all ready." Clara handed them to Gudrun with a smile. "I think you'll be pleased. I know we were quite taken with the shop, weren't we, Johanna?"

Angel's fussing was escalating with each passing minute. Though her mother tried soothing her, shifting her weight from one foot to the other, Angel would have none of it.

"I need to go feed her, then we can talk." She fled up the stairs to the nursery and settled into the rocking chair. Once the baby was happily nursing, she let her mind roam back to what she had seen. The well-stocked shop, the house just big enough for her and her children, a fenced backyard for them to play in, even a tree where she could hang a swing. There was a pasture for the horse and a cow, if she should want one. Miss Sharon had talked about the garden plot buried under the snow and the lilacs bordering the fence.

The desire to make a home in this place filled her, and her heart ached with longing. Never in her entire life had she felt such peace as within the walls of this house and she knew she could carry that feeling over to Miss Sharon's shop. Couldn't she? Could she leave her other life behind forever, could she close the door on the senseless brutality? To those who asked, couldn't she say she was a widow? Perhaps Mr. Carlson died in the blizzard or of an illness, an accident? So often she'd wished him dead.

Was it so wrong to want a new life? To provide a safe home for her children?

She stroked Angel's rounded cheek. "Oh, child, you have

no idea what your life could have been. Do I dare stop here? Will we be safe? Can I—we—live a lie?"

She ignored the voice of her conscience whispering in her ear and, after rocking Angel to sleep, she lay the baby in the cradle and made her way back down the stairs. She could hear people talking in the parlor so she turned in through the double doors and paused.

Caleb and Dag were leaning against the fireplace mantel, deep in a discussion over something upon which they did not agree. They were enjoying every moment of the argument. Caleb pounded one fist in the palm of the other hand for emphasis. Dag threw back his head, laughing and shaking his head at the same time.

Sitting close together on the horsehair sofa, Mrs. Norgaard and Clara had their heads together over some papers in the lamplight.

Mrs. Olson nodded to Johanna as she brought in a tray with cups of coffee. "Supper will be ready in a few minutes but I thought you might like these for starters." She set the tray down on the coffee table and picked up a plate of melted cheese on tiny squares of toasted bread and began passing it around.

Caleb saw Johanna when he turned to accept one of the appetizers. The smile that broke over his face made her heart leap in response. As he crossed the room to her, she had to smile back, it was only polite after all, and besides, her face refused to do anything else.

"How is our Angel today?" Such a simple question and he asked it every time they met.

"Sleeping now but she'll be awake again after supper." Perhaps he really did come only to see the children.

"Good, good."

When had he taken her hand? How could the warmth of one man's hand signify peace and another's spell only hate?

Or rage. She shivered at the thought.

"Can I get you a shawl or something? Surely there is a draft here, come over by the fire."

When she tried to withdraw her hand, he tugged it instead and led her toward the fire. "No, no, I am fine."

Dag obligingly moved over. "Here, I am sorry for hogging the warmth. You'd think I'd get my fill of fire with the forge and all but on a cold night like tonight, nothing feels better than a crackling fireplace, even though the furnace heats the house."

Johanna took the place they offered her, right in the middle. The two tall and broad-shouldered men made her feel tiny—and safe. She took the coffee cup Caleb handed her and sipped, closing her eyes in bliss. With the fire warming her back and the coffee her insides, she still felt his undeniable warmth even though they were not close enough to be touching. At the mention of Miss Sharon, Johanna rejoined the conversation.

"The shop appears to be financially stable, with sufficient inventory and fairly low overhead," Mrs. Norgaard was saying. "I'd be sorry for Soldahl to lose a business such as this. Our women need nice things without having to go to Fargo or Grand Forks."

"What's wrong with the Sears and Roebuck Catalogue?" Caleb pointed to his shirt. "Seems good enough to me, I wear their clothes all the time."

"So do a lot of other people and not only clothes but household goods and even farm machinery. They are providing a fine service, but. . ." Gudrun looked over her glasses. "If we all bought from the catalogue, we wouldn't need any businesses in Soldahl. All we'd have would be a post office, a train station, and a grain elevator." Her tart reply made the men chuckle.

"And a bank?" Caleb winked at Johanna.

The teasing and laughter between these good friends still seemed strange to her. There had been so little levity in her life. She had yet to join in; she could never think of anything to say.

"Now the saloon, that is what really draws the farmers and the ranchers in. We couldn't do without a saloon."

"I suppose you'd like for Johanna to open one of those?" Eyes flashed behind the glasses.

"No, no, just stating a fact." Caleb raised his hands in mock surrender. "You are right, the dressmaking shop is important to the well-being of the residents of Soldahl and the surrounding countryside."

"Quit your funnin' and come and eat." Mrs. Olson ordered from the doorway. "Henry and I be waiting for you."

Guilt that she'd left her son to the good graces of Mrs. Olson made Johanna take a step forward. She should have been in the kitchen helping prepare the meal instead of lazing around in the parlor. What was the matter with her, getting ahead of her station like that? The thought plagued her, easily shattering the sense of peace she'd been harboring. She set her empty coffee cup on the tray, but before she could pick it up, Caleb beat her to it.

"I'll just take this back to the kitchen and join you in the dining room."

Once again he caught her off guard. Being taken care of like this could become a habit. Would it be possible for her and the sheriff to remain friends? She'd heard stories of men leaving their families behind and starting new lives in the West. Could she do it too?

But, Johanna, a voice seemed to whisper in her ear, *all your life you've told the truth. Can you live a lie now?*

I already am, she thought. *Surely one more won't make any difference.*

fourteen

"So, do you think you would like to own the dressmaking shop?"

Johanna stared across the desk to the woman sitting erectly in the chair behind it. Gudrun clasped her hands on the blotter in front of her and looked over the rim of her glasses. The silence of the office felt as thick as before a thunderstorm, yet the twinkle in the faded eyes promised the freshness of spring rain.

"I—I. . ." Johanna blinked and started again. "You know I would like to, that isn't the problem. I have no, or rather, so little money." She'd earned a few dollars sewing for others. Shaking her head, she continued. "And I have nothing to barter."

"You have yourself and the skill of your mind and hands. I have watched you as you deal with others and you deal fairly, you understand how to set a price for your work. In my mind those are the attributes of a good businesswoman. The bank is willing to loan you the money based on those things. Those and the fact that the shop itself has made money in the past and is filling a need in the community."

"The bank—or you?"

"The bank, on my recommendation." Gudrun leaned forward. "You want a new life, why not here where you already have friends to help you get started?"

Johanna closed her eyes and sighed. *Is this what I am supposed to do? Dear God, I've been asking for an answer, is this it?* "Why not? You are right but I feel like I'm

111

standing on a high cliff and about to jump off."

"Just so you don't feel like someone is pushing you off. I am so certain I am right that at times I get a bit heavy-handed, at least that's what some of my friends tell me." The twinkle brightened. "That is a failing of mine for which I've had to ask forgiveness more than once. But in your case, I feel so strongly this is the right move, that the shop will be good for you and you for it, that I can't help but push. Your buying it will make everyone happy, including Miss Sharon and her George. What a wedding gift we are giving them. They'll be able to leave sooner than they had hoped."

Johanna let the words roll over her. She heard them, but for the life of her, she couldn't respond. She, Mrs. Raymond Carlson, Johanna, would own a dressmaking shop in the town of Soldahl, North Dakota. She would live there in that lovely little house with her two children and people would come to her to order their dresses and fine linens. And hats too, she added as an afterthought. She'd never made a real hat, only those she knit. *But I can do it, I know I can.*

With each thought she could feel her spine straightening and her shoulders squaring. *I will sign the papers Mrs. Johanna Carlson and that will be the end of that.* The day she signed the papers would be the day for her new life to begin. Not that it hadn't already but that wouldmake it official.

"When will we—what is the next step?"

"If you are in agreement, as soon as a contract is ready, we will meet with Hopstead so you can sign it. The wedding is on Saturday and Miss Sharon said she could be moved out by Sunday. You will have to get together with her so she can show you where everything is. I think she would like to leave much of her furniture so she doesn't have to pay to ship it to Montana but that is something you can discuss with her."

Johanna could feel her hands begin to shake so she clenched

them into fists and buried them in her lap. Soon even her lips
were shaking. Surely Mrs. Norgaard could hear her heels
clicking on the floor. What in the world was she doing? Bor-
rowing such an enormous amount of money from a bank and
from a friend and thinking she could have a business of her
own? What in the world possessed her to think she could do
such a thing? What would Raymond say, that is, providing he
ever found out? And her mother and father, why they would
roll over in their graves.

You're afraid, a little voice whispered in her ear. *Scared
spitless,* she wanted to scream back. And with just cause.

"You know, my dear, my husband, God rest his soul, used
to say that when you had God as a partner, you didn't need
to be afraid or worried because you had the best partner
possible. I think that applies to all areas of our lives, both
business and everyday living. It sure has helped me through
many decisions. I always pray, knowing God will answer."

"Thank you, I'll remember that." Johanna got to her feet.
"I think I better go check on Angel and I have some mending to do for a lady. Thank you for all you have done for us.
God surely counts on you as one of His servants." She darted
from the room before the moisture welling up overcame
her parched throat and spilled out her eyes.

❧

"We found your wagon," Caleb said a couple of nights later
when he'd come for supper. "You'd gotten way off the road
and down in a low spot. The drifts just covered it over until
this bit of a thaw." He shook his head. "Thank God you
had the presence of mind to get on the horse and let him
bring you in."

Johanna nodded. She thanked God every day for the miracle
of their rescue. "Thank you, Sheriff." Henry tugged at her
sleeve and pointed to Sam. The dog wagged his tail. "I know,
we have Sam to thank too." She put both hands around the

dog's face and looked directly into his eyes. "Sam, you are the best dog in the whole world." Stroking his soft head, she wondered what would happen to Henry when Sam returned to his own house. Surely the sheriff didn't intend to give up his dog forever. So many things to think about.

"Thought I'd take your horse out tomorrow and drag the wagon free and bring it in."

"You need some help?" Dag asked.

"Yup, could use some." He looked over at Johanna with a smile deepening the creases at the outside of his eyes. "We'll put it in the lean-to of the barn at your house. I already took some hay over there and a sack of grain for your horse. If you want you can buy milk from the Ericksons, on the next block and one house in. Their cow freshened so they have plenty, and they usually sell a few eggs too. I'd bring some in for you but my hens quit laying about the time that you arrived. They didn't like that blizzard any better'n the rest of us."

"Thank you." Johanna thoughts flew to the boxes of dishes and pans, sheets, and quilts Mrs. Olson and Gudrun had been packing for her. They said it was all stuff no longer used in the big house but to Johanna it was riches unheard of.

Three more days and she could build a fire in her own cookstove, tuck Henry into what would be his own bed, and work as late into the evening as she desired. She would pay the mortgage off long before its time if there were any way humanly possible.

&

The whole town turned out for the wedding and to send the bride and groom on their way. After the service, they greeted everyone, cut the cake, and ran for the train.

"I'm so glad you came to take over for me," Miss Sharon, now Mrs. Drummond, called to Johanna from the steps of the train. "Thank you, thank you everyone." She waved again as the "All aboard" echoed down the track.

"So, would you like us to help you move in now?" Caleb stood at Johanna's shoulder, Henry between them.

"Really?" Johanna fingered the keys given her just before the bridal couple boarded the train. She'd never had keys to anything, let alone a house and shop.

"Why not? It isn't like you have a trainload of stuff to move. We'll hitch up your horse and bring him 'round to the mansion. I heard tell that there are a few others with items to help you get started, the Moens for sure." Caleb hefted Henry up on his shoulders. "Let's get to it." He waved to Dag who was just handing Gudrun into the sleigh. "I'm ready anytime you are."

Dag returned the wave. "I'll meet you at my house then."

"How about you and Henry stop at your new house? You can look around and decide where you want things while we load up."

Johanna felt caught up in the middle of a twister. "But. . ."

"No problem, Mrs. Olson and Clara know what is to go, they'll probably beat us over there. Gudrun can watch Angel until we get things a mite more settled, then we're all invited back for supper. I think Mrs. Olson had this all planned, she just likes to let the rest of us think we're in charge." He took her arm and, all the while he talked, they made their way up the now bare boardwalk to stop right in front of the picket fence surrounding the weathered building. He pushed open the gate and waved her through.

Johanna stopped halfway up the walk. An aged oak tree spread bare branches over the western side of the house, promising the cool rustle of leaves and shade during the hot summer. One branch cried for a rope swing. Under the snowbanks, Miss Sharon had said, slept hollyhock and pansies, daisies and daffodils. Johanna closed her eyes to imagine a pink climbing rose twining up the porch post and across the lintel. She'd have a rocker on the front porch and maybe a pot of flowers, bright and cheery. Miss Sharon's sign would come down to be replaced by. . .

Her eyes flew open. "What am I going to call my shop?"

"*Johanna's* sounds good to me, better than *Carlson's.*" His voice came from right to the left of her ear. She could feel the heat of him, even through her wool coat. The temptation to lean back and let his strong body hold her up sent warmth flying into her face. She could feel it, like a windburn. Almost in desperation, she fumbled in her pocket for the set of keys. With them securely in her hand, she led the way up the steps, across the porch, and to the storm door. She took a deep breath before opening the door and sliding a shaking key into the hole. She turned it, heard the click, and, after shooting an imploring look, put her hand on the knob.

Please, Lord, let this be the best move ever. Please bless us and our new home. She took another deep breath, let it out, and turned the doorknob. The bell tinkled over the opening door, a welcome sound, and she stepped inside. Sure enough, all the fabrics were as she'd seen before. The room looked like Miss Sharon might be in back, working on a garment for a customer. Johanna fought down the urge to call "Is anyone home?" and took two more steps into the room.

"You'll be all right here?" Caleb's deep voice broke the stillness.

"Ja, we will." She whispered her answer, afraid if she spoke too loud, the spell would break. At that moment she slammed the door on that former life, one she would put out of her mind and heart forever to begin this life anew.

"I'll be going then. We should be back within an hour or so."

She turned and looked up to the man who had set her son down when they came through the door. The low ceiling didn't allow for a tall man with a boy on his shoulders.

"Thank you, Caleb. I cannot say it enough."

"You just look around and decide where you want things so's we can all help put them away when we get here."

"I will." She crossed the room again to let him out the door, her very own door, to her very own home and shop. "Good-bye." She turned to find Henry right behind her, his eyes huge in his face. His lower lip quivered.

"What is it, son?" How she wished he would talk. Life with him would be so much easier.

A tear trembled on his lashes.

"Did you want to go with the sheriff?" He nodded. A light burst in her mind. The dog, of course, the dog. "Sam will come back with him. He couldn't go to the church with us, you know." How she hoped Caleb would leave his dog with her son just a few more days. Enough time to get him settled in this new place. Come spring, perhaps some-one would have a puppy to give away.

He brushed the tear away and heaved a sigh of obvious relief. Then, taking her hand, he joined her in her explora-tion of their home. Together they opened cupboard doors and pulled out drawers. They located the door to the base-ment and decided not to go down there until they had a lamp. While the house was lit with gas lights, she wasn't even sure how to operate them, let alone find one in the dark. Up the narrow stairs to the second floor she threw open the door to a room under the eaves.

"This will be your room, Henry. See, your own bed, and look out the window. You'll be able to watch the horse and our cow, when we get one, out in the field." She plopped down on the bed. "What do you think?"

Henry stood at the window, then turned with a smile on his face. With a deep sigh, he ran and threw himself into her lap, burying his face in her skirts.

Johanna stroked his head. "I know, son, I know. We can

both feel safe here." She lifted his chin and kissed his fore-head. "Come, let's see the rest."

They'd only gotten as far as the workroom when the bell tinkled in the shop.

"Mrs. Carlson?" A woman's voice, one Johanna didn't recognize, called.

"Ja, I am here." She dusted off her hands and pushed the curtain aside to greet her guest. "Mrs. Moen, what a nice surprise."

"I was afraid you might not be here yet, but we brought a few things to help you set up housekeeping." She opened the door and called, "Come on in!"

Within minutes the room was full of Moens, each bearing a gift of some kind, a nine-patch quilt, some canned fruit, a loaf of bread, butter in a butter mold, a braided rug rolled under Mary's arm, and finally Reverend Moen entered carrying a rocking chair.

"Where's Angel?" Mary asked.

Johanna turned to the girl. "Mrs. Norgaard is keeping her."

"Oh." The girl's face fell. "I was hoping to hold her."

"Where do you want me to put this?" asked John Moen.

"In here by the fire," Ingeborg answered, motioning him into the kitchen. She found places for each of their offerings and kept on being the shepherd as the wagon pulled up from the mansion. The children helped bring in the boxes and, as soon as Clara made it through the door, she began putting food in the pie safe out on the back porch, dishes on the cupboard shelves, and handed Henry the broom.

"That goes out on the back porch, I imagine." When Dag brought in a rather large box, she showed him the stairway going up. "That's linens so we can make the beds."

Johanna had never felt so loved and useless in her life. Here were her friends doing all the things she should be doing and that would take hours. They were finished before sundown.

"Now, isn't this just the nicest?" Ingeborg Moen clasped her hands and gazed around the kitchen. A teakettle now steamed on the stove and the braided rug lay in front of the sink that sprouted a red pump on the left. A red geranium with a white eye graced the kitchen window sill and two dishtowels hung on the rack on the side of the cupboard. Henry sat in the rocker with Sam at his feet and one of the Moen children kept the chair moving.

"I'm sure Mrs. Olson has supper ready so we best be going."

"And Angel is probably screaming her head off." Johanna grabbed her and Henry's coats off the pegs by the back door and bundled him into them. How could she have forgotten Angel in the midst of all this bounty? Poor baby certainly wouldn't accept such an excuse.

"We can all load in the wagon, then I'll take the Moens home when I bring you back," Caleb said with a nod. He signaled them all to the door and, once outside, closed it behind him.

"Shouldn't I lock it?" Johanna fingered the key in her pocket.

"Whatever for?" Caleb stopped with one foot on the lower step. "No one around here locks doors."

"But it was locked when we came."

"That was only because Miss Sharon wasn't sure how long before you'd move in." He took her arm. "Besides, it seemed more official this way. Come on, supper's waiting."

Feeling carried along by a rushing river, Johanna joined the others in the wagon. They really should have runners on it in this snow and ice but the horse pulled it forward anyway.

They could hear Angel crying as soon as their feet hit the front step.

fifteen

Bright and early Monday morning her first customer walked in the door.

Johanna laid Angel back in the cradle Gudrun had loaned her for downstairs and pushed back the curtains to the shop. "Good morning, how can I help you?"

"I would like a new outfit for Easter. Miss Sharon said she wasn't taking any orders and that I should come back to talk with you."

Johanna extended her hand. "I am Johanna Carlson and I will be glad to make you a new garment for Easter. Do you have an idea what you would like?"

The customer took Johanna's hand and shook it vigorously. "I am Mrs. Ernest Hopstead, wife of the bank manager. I believe you already have the beginnings of a fine reputation here in Soldahl. Miss Sharon usually let me look through the Godey's books until I found something I liked and then she talked me into what might look better." She gestured to her rounded figure. "But what she came up with was always stylish. I will need a hat to go with it."

Johanna could feel her heart hopping up and down like a frightened bunny. *Dear Lord, please give me wisdom.* "Have you looked around at the new spring materials? Miss Sharon had a goodly stock put in before she left for which I am exceedingly grateful." She studied the woman before her. A blue would like nice with her faded blond coloring. She crossed the room to a bolt of watered blue silk, not even daring to look at the price marked on it. "I think this would be lovely on you." Draping a length of fabric over the woman's shoulder, she moved her to stand in front of the full-length mirror.

"Oh, that *is* nice." Mrs. Hopstead slid gentle fingers over the sleek fabric. "And silk rustles so prettily too. Let's do it in that and now to find a dress I like."

Johanna sat her in front of a round table with a fringed cloth that swept the floor. The three latest fashion books already lay on the table. "I'll let you look and be right back." She no more got back to the kitchen to check on Angel, who was now sleeping, and Henry, who was playing with a horse and rider Caleb had given him, than the bell over the door tinkled again. By noon she had two dress orders for Easter and a set of monogrammed sheets for a wedding present.

By the end of the day she had her work cut out for her. Two more women had come in, one ordering three summer dresses for herself and two each for her two daughters.

"Make Abigail's, that's the one in blue, extra nice because it's time she caught a beau," the woman confided.

"Oh, I will," Johanna promised. "You'll all come by for a fitting the middle of next week?"

The other needed some alterations and wondered if Johanna could come to her house to fit them. With a smile on her face and panic in her heart, Johanna agreed.

She put the children down for their naps and began cutting the watered silk. She'd talked Mrs. Hopstead into tucks down the front of the bodice rather than gathered lace like the picture showed, knowing that lace would make the woman's bosom larger, which it certainly didn't need. She'd found the card file with Miss Sharon's comments on her customers as to what looked good, their measurements, and what they had purchased in the past. Carefully she had measured the woman to make sure the size hadn't changed. It had, making her grateful for her caution. Wisely she kept the numbers to herself, quickly realizing the woman had a vain streak about a foot wide.

The bell tinkled again and she left her cutting table to see who it was. "Clara, how nice of you to stop by." Relief poured through her at the sight of her friend. "Come in, let me put the coffeepot on."

"I hear you've been busy today." Clara pulled off her gloves and removed her coat.

"Ja, how did you know?"

"Oh, a little bird told me. I'm so happy for you, I could bust."

"Don't do that, Dag would get very upset with me." Johanna smiled in answer to the beam Clara sent her. "You are looking mighty happy today."

"I know, I have the most wonderful secret but I can't tell Dag yet until I am absolutely sure."

"You are with child."

Clara nodded. "I—we've been waiting so long and I was beginning to be afraid it wouldn't happen. Gudrun kept telling me all in God's time, but I never have been the most patient person." She looked over to the fine cottons. "You know all those baby things we made, I think that is what turned the trick."

Johanna chuckled along with her friend. "Come, we must have some of Mrs. Olson's apple cake to celebrate."

Clara hung back, wandering over to the delicate cottons. "I was wondering if you would make us a baptismal gown for him or her. Of course Dag will say it is a him but we both know how important girls are too."

"I would love to sew that for you, and at least you don't have to have it done by Easter." Together they made their way to the kitchen, Clara admiring the silk on the cutting table on the way.

"I will need some things let out soon and I thought maybe you would make me some others with an expanding waist or no waist at all. I haven't even told Gudrun and Mrs. Olson yet."

"Of course." Johanna rattled the coals and dropped in a couple of pieces of small wood to get the fire going faster. She pulled the coffeepot to the front. "This will only take a minute. You are the first one to drink coffee with me in my brand-new house." She took cups and saucers out of the cupboard, admiring the small stack of dishes as she did so. All of this was hers. For the first time in years she had things of her own, things no one would throw and break, pretty things that she didn't have to hide.

She'd just shown Clara to the door and gone back to cutting when Angel began to whimper. When Johanna finished cutting out the skirt panel, Angel was in full cry. Henry made his way down the stairs into the kitchen and stood at her knee as she settled Angel to nursing.

The bell over the door tinkled again. "Anybody home?" A man's voice called.

"Yes, Caleb, we're in the kitchen." She should have put the closed sign on the door if she wanted to nurse her baby in peace. She threw the baby quilt over her shoulder, already feeling the red climb up her neck. A man walking in on a woman nursing her baby just wasn't proper. "Henry, you go bring the sheriff back here, okay?"

The boy blinked sleepy eyes but nodded. When he heard a dog whine, he flew through the curtained door.

Johanna listened as the man and dog greeted the child. How good it would be to hear a childish voice responding. As a baby, he had made gurgling noises and answered her

with coos and smiles. He'd begun to talk too so she knew
he could. But ever since that night, he'd never spoken again,
learning instead how to disappear into the woodwork so no
one would notice him.

With Caleb he was a different child.

"Sam said he was getting mighty lonely for his friend here,
so I thought maybe I would loan him to you for a couple of
days, help you get settled and all, that is, if you want a dog
under foot." Caleb had removed his coat and hat and hung
them on the coat tree near the front door. He ran a hand
back over his hair to smooth it down. The gesture tugged at
her heart. Such a fine man he was, both in appearance and
in heart.

"I don't mind at all. I know Henry missed him but I explained you needed him too."

"And that made it all right?"

She shook her head. "But he understood and endured."

"I think for such a small one, he's endured a great deal."
Caleb pulled a chair out from the kitchen table and turned it
so he could sit with his arms crossed on the back.

If you only knew. She hoped the thought didn't show on
her face. It was hard to keep secrets from this man; he was
too used to reading faces for the truth.

Angel finished her meal and let out a loud burp. Johanna
rose to her feet and excused herself so she could put her
dress back to rights. The baby waved her arms and smiled
up at her mother, a milky bubble caught at the corner of her
mouth. Johanna snuggled her close and kissed the downy
hair, coming in darker than the baby fuzz.

When they returned to the kitchen, Caleb sat cross-legged
on the floor, rolling a ball to Henry. "I just happened to see
this at the Mercantile and thought that a boy needs a ball.
I'm thinking that when spring comes, we'll have to put up a

swing from that oak branch out there. God made it perfectly
for such a thing."

"You've been reading my mind." Johanna spread a quilt
on the floor and laid Angel on her tummy in the middle.
She ignored the swipe of a tongue from Sam on the baby's
cheek and went about warming the coffee again. "Would
you like to stay for supper?"

"No, I better get on home, I have chores to do and. . ."

Johanna could almost finish his sentence: ". . .and it
wouldn't be proper for the sheriff to be seen leaving the
seamstress's home after dark."

"Another time then." She turned with the coffeepot in
one hand and a cup and saucer in the other. "I'll serve this
at the table." She poured two cups of coffee and a glass of
milk for Henry, and then put a plate of cookies on the table,
thanks to Mrs. Moen, and laid a couple of spoons in front
of Angel.

Before she could sit down, Caleb had pulled her chair out
for her. She took her seat, the heat rising up her face again.
Why did this man have such an amazing effect on her? And
what could she do about it? While her heart said one thing,
her head overruled it. There was nothing she could do but
ignore her emotions.

On Sunday he showed up to escort her to church. She'd
spent the week sewing far into the night and rising early in
the morning to continue her work. Every day she thanked
the good Lord for the sewing machine that whirred away
the hours. The fittings went well, in fact everything was
going so well. How could life be so good to someone who
was living a lie?

Reverend Moen's sermon verse, ". . .and the truth shall
set you free," made her wince.

Caleb looked over at her, Henry sound asleep on his lap.

Did he know? Did he suspect? The urge to tell someone her story ate at her for the rest of the week. Should she talk to Reverend Moen? She knew of his kind heart but he would have to abide by the Scriptures. Gudrun? Of any of her friends, she would be the one.

She finished the last stitch in the last Easter dress on Saturday morning, just after dawn lightened the eastern sky. While the sun was not yet up, she went to stand at her kitchen window to watch the band of soft silver deepen to gold and then flame into pinks and purples as the golden disc arched above the horizon. Perhaps they would have good weather for Easter. The thaw had been dripping off the icicles the last four days.

As on the other mornings, her prayer was the same. "Dear Lord, thank You for what You have given me and now, please show me what to do." The plea had nothing to do with her day's work. She set bread dough to rising, rolled out and baked a batch of sour cream cookies, and was well into scrubbing the kitchen floor when Sam and Henry snuck down the stairs.

"Breakfast will be ready as soon as I'm done here. Why don't you let Sam out in the meantime and then go get dressed?" At his nod, she went back to her bucket of soapy water. By the time she'd mopped up the last brush of water, she could hear Angel begin to fuss in the cradle she'd moved into the other room. Sam yipped at the back door, Henry meandered back down the stairs, and Angel passed from fussing to demanding. Like the time and tides, babies waited for no one.

Several people dropped by that day with gifts of food or small household items, welcoming her to the community and making her feel a part of Soldahl. Each time the bell tinkled, Sam and Henry would run to the door to see who was there. Johanna knew they were waiting for Caleb. By the time dusk fell, she could feel her spirits falling along with it. Though it was hard to admit, she'd been looking forward to his visit as much as the two who now had their noses plastered against the front window.

"Supper's ready," she called.

Just as they sat down and had said grace, the doorbell chimed again. Sam took off, his toenails making him skid on the freshly waxed floor. When Henry started to follow, Johanna shook her head. "You sit here and eat while the food is hot." She could tell from the dog's yips who it was. Henry's mouth turned down and he hung his head.

"Sorry I'm so late but the train didn't get here on time." While he spoke, he set a large square box down on the floor. Sam sniffed it and sat in front of the sheriff, like he was waiting for a description of the contents of the box. Henry turned in his chair and stared from the box to the sheriff's face and back again.

"I know this is early but I wanted to give him something for Easter." Caleb shrugged. "I know, I'm as bad as a kid, can't wait to open boxes." He raised an eyebrow. "Is it all right—for him to have it now, I mean?"

Johanna nodded. What else could she do? The look on Henry's face tore her heart out of her chest and plastered it on her sleeve. At her nod again, he darted across the room and placed his hands on the box. Looking up at the man above him, the boy needed no words to voice his plea.

"Here, you want me to help you?" At the boy's nod, Caleb took a pocketknife from his pant's pocket and cut the strings. With eyes as big as dinner plates, Henry pulled open the crossed sections of the box flaps and peered inside.

"Yes, that's for you," Caleb answered the unspoken question. "Go ahead, take it out." He tipped the box over on its side to make it easier. Henry crawled halfway inside before backing out, his hand clamped around the handle of a red wagon with bright yellow wheels inside of black rims.

Johanna shot Caleb a look of combined joy and oh-you-shouldn't-have-done-this.

Caleb raised a hand. "I know what you're thinking, but every boy needs a red wagon. Just think, this summer he'll be able to pull Angel around in it. Should keep them happy for hours while you sew away."

"I don't know how to thank you."

"Not your place. The wagon is Henry's and he's more than thanked me already. Ain't often in this world you can bring such a light of joy to a child's face. I'd pay for that privilege many times over." He folded the box closed. "You want I should put this down in the cellar?"

"No, leave it here." She pointed to a corner. "He will have a wonderful time playing in that, along with the wagon."

"Fine then, I'll see you in the morning for church."

Late that night Johanna finished stitching the lace trim to a bonnet for Angel to wear for Easter. She and Henry would make do with what they had. At the rate he was growing, what he had wouldn't be worn for much longer. When they walked into the church in the morning, they had a hard time finding a place to sit. New bonnets crowned the women's heads, leaving her feeling like a black sheep in a field of white ones. Dag finally saw them and beckoned them to the second pew. Walking with the sheriff up the center aisle, Johanna could feel eyes drilling into her back. Without turning, she could feel the whispers passed along behind gloved hands. If the residents of Soldahl hadn't noticed the attention he paid to her before, they certainly did now.

She took her place next to Clara and sat Henry between

her and Caleb.

"Christ is risen!" announced Reverend Moen.

"He is risen indeed!" responded the congregation. As the service continued with the reading of the women at the sepulcher, Johanna felt the tears gather as Mary pleaded with the man to tell her where they'd laid the body. She contemplated how much Christ had done for Mary and the others, and for her. How could she repay Him?

She knew the answer. By not living a lie. She quickly focused on the words of the Gospel and tried to ignore that silent voice for the rest of the service. It wasn't fair. Was God asking this of her? To go back? To leave her new life? Surely He wouldn't send her back.

After church those invited to the mansion for dinner boarded wagons and buggies, ducking under cover to keep the mist off them. While the sun had cracked the horizon, clouds had returned, but at least it was too warm to snow.

The long table held places for Caleb, Johanna, Reverend and Mrs. Moen, and Will Dunfey, Dag's assistant. Another table was set for the Moen children and Henry.

"He'll be fine with me," Mary, the eldest daughter reassured Johanna. "Come on, Henry, we can have more fun in the kitchen."

"No doubt," Reverend Moen whispered.

"Will you say the grace, John?" Gudrun asked from her place at the foot of the table. Dag sat at the head with Clara on his right. When they bowed their heads in a moment of silence, Johanna heard the voice again. Surely if she told anyone, they would think her mad. She concentrated on the prayer and the voice faded.

Course followed course, with Mrs. Olson carrying platters and bowls and encouraging everyone— "Eat up, there's plenty more where this came from."

"There certainly is, she's been cooking and baking for three days." Dag said when the cook left the room to bring in another steaming platter.

"Well, I for one don't intend to let any of this go to waste." Caleb passed the platter of sliced ham to Johanna. The conversation flowed along with the food. When Mrs. Olson swung open the kitchen door, laughter could be heard from the children. John raised an eyebrow but settled back down at a head shake from Gudrun.

"They aren't hurting anything and this old house needs the joy of children's laughter."

Johanna looked across the table at Clara, an eyebrow raised in question. A slight shake of the head and a quickly hidden smile said she hadn't told the others yet. Sharing such a wonderful secret gave Johanna a warm glow around her heart. Never had she had friends like these. Would they still be her friends when she told them the whole story?

Later that evening when Caleb took her home, he stopped on the front porch.

"Would you like to come in?"

He shook his head. "I better not, but I have something important to ask you."

She looked into his eyes, shaded by the dark and his hat's wide brim. "Yes."

He cleared his throat and sucked in a deep breath. "I. . . you. . . ah. . .I need your permission to court you and I certainly hope you feel the same." The words came out in a rush.

Johanna felt her heart collapse at that moment.

sixteen

"What do you mean you don't want to see me anymore?"

"Just that." Johanna twisted her hands in knots.

Caleb stared at her, his heart about to leap from his chest. Had he misread all the signs? Surely he wouldn't feel this way if he hadn't felt she did too. All these years, he'd never even escorted anyone to church, or the socials or. . . .

He slammed his fist against the doorjamb. Johanna jumped as if she'd been shot.

"I'm sorry, that was uncalled for." He stared at her, trying to read what was behind her face and in her heart.

She refused to meet his eyes.

"Johanna, I can't believe you are talking like this." He wanted to take her hands, enfold her in his arms, protect her from whatever monster was hiding inside.

"I'm sorry, Caleb, that's just the way it has to be." Her voice sounded lost.

Caleb looked around the shop, as if hoping a message might jump at him from the walls or the piles of material. The night before he had not pressed her for an answer. He'd just hightailed it off her porch as if his tail were on fire. Now as he glanced over at the curtained doorway to her workroom he could see Henry peeking through the crack. What a fool he had been. He knew loud voices scared the daylights out of the child and more than once he'd seen Johanna hide within herself when a man raised his voice. And here he'd done both.

"Good-bye, Caleb." She turned and, shoulders squared

beneath her dark dress, pushed through the curtain.

He could hear her comforting Henry in a gentle voice.

Caleb crammed his hat back on his head and gave the door a satisfying slam. Halfway to the street, he turned right and headed west to the main part of town, his boots kicking up slush in his long strides. For his own benefit he recited in his head a litany of names that applied to one Caleb Stensrude.

"Good morning, Sheriff," someone called.

He heard but pounded on. He could feel curious eyes drilling into his back but his stride never shortened. By the time he'd reached the Ericksons' driveway, his chest pumped like a bellows and sweat slimed his hat band. He'd covered over three miles.

The sun beat down on his shoulders yet he could feel the ice creeping over his heart. "Dear God, why?" He looked toward the heavens. "Why?" This time a dog barked, the sound carrying over a still-snowbound prairie.

"I prayed over this, thought I was doing what You wanted." He wiped the sweat off his brow with the back of his hand and unbuttoned his sheepskin jacket. Between the sun and the hard walk he no longer needed that. He shook his head and snorted. "No fool like an old fool." He turned around and started back. The way he had stormed around, probably half the town was talking about him now.

When he reached the wrought-iron fence surrounding the Norgaard mansion—no one called it the Weinlander house even though all knew Dag owned it now—he paused. Perhaps Gudrun knew what was keeping Johanna from him. For certain she'd heard about his rampage through the streets of Soldahl.

Here, like some lovesick bull, he'd been thinking this might be one of the happiest days of his life. Women! He punched the doorbell with unnecessary force.

"Why, Caleb, what a nice surprise, we haven't seen so much of you lately." Clara smiled up at him, the twinkle in her eye going along with her teasing. "Come on in." She stepped back and beckoned him inside.

Caleb removed his Stetson and held it in front of him with both hands. Now that he was actually here, he wanted to be anywhere else. "Is Gudrun in?"

"Of course, she's in her office." Her look this time reminded him of his mother. "Something's wrong, isn't it?"

He nodded. "You might want to join us. She might have let you in on her secret."

Clara turned her head a bit. "She?" She studied Caleb briefly. "I'll go ask Mrs. Olson to bring in some coffee. You go right on." She turned toward the kitchen. "You might want to tap on the door before you go in."

Caleb watched her dart down the hall. *How in the world did I let myself in for this?* He added a few more names to those he'd already called himself and made his way through the parlor and down the hall to the office. He looked down to realize he still wore his sheepskin jacket and hadn't even hung his hat on the hall tree. *Not a good sign, son. Why don't you just hightail it home and go chop wood or something?*

But instead, he tapped on the carved walnut door.

"Come in."

Once before he'd felt just this way—the time he was summoned to the principal's office at the high school.

"Caleb, what a nice surprise." Gudrun stuck her pen back in the ink stand. "Sit down, sit down." She stood and came around the desk. "Let's sit in front of the fire, if you would be so kind as to stoke it up." All the while she spoke, she watched his face.

Once he'd put another log on, he took the wingback chair opposite hers.

"Now, tell me what's wrong."

"Can't one friend call on another without anything being wrong?" He settled his hat on his knee and studied the fire now beginning to blaze again. He sighed and slumped against the leather upholstered back.

When he finally looked up at Gudrun, her gaze met his with compassion.

"Mrs. Olson will bring the coffee in a few minutes." Clara said after tapping at the door and entering.

Gudrun looked at Caleb with a question.

"It's all right. I asked Clara to join us." He traced the rim of the crown of his hat with one finger. "You see. . .I. . .ah . . .no, this isn't working." He clapped his hands on the chair arms and started to rise.

"Sit, Caleb."

Steel with a velvet covering. He now knew what that meant. He sat.

Clara pulled up a chair and took her place.

He caught a look that passed between them, a look of question and concern all wrapped up together. He sucked in a deep breath and let the words out in a whoosh. "Do you know any reason why Johanna would not want me to court her?"

"Oh, no, I was afraid of that."

He stared at the older woman, willing her to go on.

She shook her head and looked at Clara who did the same. "She's never confided in me," Gudrun began, "but I know there is something in her past that she keeps carefully hidden. I have an idea what it is but that is all." She stared into the fire. "We've all noticed how she mentions nothing about her life before you found her at your gate. That is strange in itself. But I've also seen her flinch or duck away when a man raises his voice or moves too quickly."

"I know, I've seen that too. You think she's running from a wife-beating husband? What with Henry being so scared and all?"

"I can't see her committing some crime, not Johanna. She's as honest as the day is long." Clara tapped her fingers together.

"But she was definitely on the run. I was surprised when she agreed to buy the dress shop." Gudrun looked up at the tap on the door. "Come in."

After Mrs. Olson fussed with the coffee tray and left, she continued. "What happened today?"

"I. . .well, you know I've not been hiding my interest in her. Why those two tykes of hers are dear to me as my own. That Angel could make the devil himself smile."

"Let alone our dear sheriff." Clara handed the coffee cups around.

"Yeah, well, be that as it may, today I asked her if I could come courting. I thought I ought to make sure she knew my intentions were honorable."

"Of course." Gudrun sipped her coffee.

"She turned me down flat, said she didn't think she should see me anymore. Can you beat that?" He could feel his heart start thumping against his ribs again at the memory. "So I thought to ask you if you knew any reason for such a thing."

"I'm glad you did. I think it's time we got to the bottom of this—for both your sakes. Living a lie will eat away at one 'til there's nothing left."

"There's something going on for sure," Clara added. "I've seen her look at you when you weren't paying attention. That wasn't the look of someone who didn't care, even Dag noticed."

Caleb leaned back in his chair. So he wasn't nuts, he hadn't been misreading the woman.

Gudrun set her cup and saucer down with a click. "So the question is, what can we do?"

Caleb nearly smiled at the mention of "we." That was one thing about Gudrun, she didn't let any grass grow under her feet. When something needed doing, no matter how hard or distasteful, she got right to it. Maybe coming here wasn't such a bad idea after all. Caleb stood and took up the poker, moving the logs around whether they needed it or not. He set the brass screen back in place to protect the fading oriental rug and returned to his seat, only to get back up and lean against the mantel.

He crossed to the table where the tray sat and poured himself another cup of coffee. He crossed to the table again and picked a cookie off the plate. About ready to reach for the poker again, he ordered himself back to the chair.

"That's better. You're acting like a cat on a hot stove." Gudrun's smile took any sting out of her words. She nodded. "Guess it's about time I go over and order a new summer dress from Johanna. That ought to give us a splendid opportunity to talk, don't you think?" She looked up at Clara who nodded and smiled widely.

"And if need be, I'll order one too. In fact, she knows I need several new things."

"I'll ask Dag to send Will over to drive the carriage tomorrow, or the sleigh, whichever. I haven't been shopping in quite some time. What do you think, Clara, do I need a new hat too?"

"I think Mrs. Johanna Carlson doesn't stand a chance."

seventeen

Johanna rubbed her forehead with weary fingers. *Why do I feel so empty? I did the right thing, I know I did.* She bent over her sewing machine, blinking to clear her eyes. Was she coming down with a cold? She blew her nose and wiped her eyes. After finishing the final seam in the skirt she was constructing, she tied off the threads and folded the waistless garment. Rubbing her aching back with one hand, she got to her feet and shoved the chair closer to the treadle machine. She should have gone to bed far earlier but the orders had stacked up and she needed the money. The first payment on her house was due soon.

She shut off the lamps and climbed the stairs to her bedroom, a kerosene lamp in hand. She checked on Henry, sound asleep with Sam lying right beside him. He wagged his tail when she patted his head.

Next, she held the light over Angel's cradle, also soundly sleeping, her little rear in the air. Johanna adjusted the quilt covering the baby and tiptoed over to her own bed. Each action seemed to take all the strength she had, as if she were slogging through deep snowdrifts. She wrapped her arms around her elbows and hugged herself, rocking back and forth to stem the sobs that threatened to tear her apart. If she weren't careful, she'd wake the baby. She shed her clothes and crawled under the covers, burying her face and her sobs in the pillow.

Waking in the morning to a baby's screaming cries did nothing for her peace of mind. "Shush, little one, your ma's right here." She changed the soaking baby and took her into bed with her for her breakfast.

That afternoon when the bell tinkled for the third or fourth time, she was losing track, she entered the shop to see Clara fingering a bolt of gingham. "Clara, how good to see you." Johanna extended her hands.

"And you." Clara took them and smiled, her gaze searching. "Gudrun wanted to come today too, but she ended up feeling a mite poorly so I came alone. Have you thought anything about some gowns for me for the months ahead?"

Johanna shook her head. "I haven't had to time to think about what to cook for dinner. While I can't afford the help, I have thought of hiring that young woman that worked for Miss Sharon." She swung their still joined hands. "Have you told Dag yet?"

Clara nodded, her eyes sparkling. "He's choosing boy names, of course. And Gudrun is ready to redecorate the nursery. Says we are finally fulfilling her heart's desire, to see children playing again in that big house."

"Here, do you have time for a cup of tea?" Johanna turned toward the workroom. "Let me put away a couple of things first. You go on in and sit down." She spun around and hurried over to the front door. After turning the lock, she pulled down a shade that said "Closed."

Clara stood over the cradle in the corner, her hands clasped to her bosom, a smile curving her mouth. "She is so beautiful." Her whisper greeted Johanna at the doorway. "Angel, that is indeed who you are." She looked up when Johanna brought the teakettle forward on the stove. "I am not surprised a bit that Caleb is so taken with her. Perhaps she reminds him of his own baby girl."

Johanna felt herself stiffen, and when she tried to swallow, her throat was dry. "D—do you take milk with your tea?"

"No, thank you, a bit of honey if you have it, otherwise

sugar." Clara crossed the room and sank into the rocking chair. "You have made such a cozy home already." She looked at the blocks Henry had left by the big box the wagon came in. "I think children's things give that feeling, don't you?"

Have you seen Caleb? Johanna's mind screamed so loudly she was afraid her visitor would cover her ears. *Did Caleb send you here?* She squashed that thought with a *Don't be silly,* and poured the boiling water over the tea leaves. Reminding herself that she had done what was best, she poured the liquid into the cups and handed one to her guest. "Why don't we sit at the table?" Her cup rattled against the saucer.

"Johanna, are you all right?" Clara studied her over the rim of her cup. "You're working too hard, aren't you?"

"No, no, I'm fine, just busy, that's all. Running a shop like this takes some getting used to, you know. I think I got lazy living in the lap of luxury like I did at your house."

Clara harrumphed and shook her head. "Lazy does not apply to you, my friend. But you look, I don't know, troubled, sad."

Angel whimpered in her cradle. *Thank You, Lord, for small favors.* Johanna pushed back her chair. "I need to change and feed her. We'll be right back." A few minutes later, settled in the rocker, Johanna kept the conversation centered on general matters, refusing to allow the personal to surface again. That was one of the bad things about good friends. They had the ability to see right through each other. And Clara was exceedingly perceptive.

Later, after playing with the baby, Clara sighed. "I really must go. We'll talk about those dresses as the time gets closer. I miss having you at the house, and Henry and Angel. It's awfully quiet again. I even miss Sam's claws ticking on the floors, silly, isn't it?"

"No, I don't think it silly at all. I'm just so grateful you call me friend."

Clara donned her coat and hat by the front door. "Just so you know that this friend is available should you ever need anything, especially someone to talk to."

"I know that, and thank you." Johanna heard Henry and the dog coming down the stairs. She leaned her head against the glass in the door, watching Clara reach the street, turn, and wave. That was one more thing. If Caleb didn't visit anymore, she would have to get his dog back to him some way. He was probably so mad at her, he'd whistle for Sam when he was outside. Surely Henry was feeling safe enough now, or was he?

The thought of the days and weeks ahead with no Caleb to come calling brought a heaviness to her chest. Why couldn't they still be friends?

⁓

On Sunday she walked to church with her children. She looked around the congregation from the rear but nowhere did she see his broad shoulders and fine head. When they left, he still had not come. Was he sick? The thought grabbed at her insides.

She forced a smile and answered the greetings of those around her. When Angel began to fuss, she excused herself and headed for home. *You will not cry!* she berated herself again and again. *You chose this path so now you must walk it—alone.*

A carriage pulled up beside her. "I know it's too late to offer you a ride, but we would love you to come for dinner." Dag's voice drew her around.

"Thanks, but not today. I have so much to do and Angel is fussing. She might be coming down with something so I think I better keep her home." Angel was fussing but only because she was hungry. Was this little white lie a terrible thing? Surely she couldn't bear it if Caleb were there. He usually came for Sunday dinner.

"I'm sorry," Clara added. "I know Gudrun would love to see you and the children. She's feeling rather housebound."

Guilt could drive arrows deeper than any bow. "Is she very sick?" *Go, no, don't go* wrestled in her mind.

"She doesn't dare be, the way Mrs. Olson is carrying on." Clara shook her head, setting the ribbons on her bonnet to bobbing. "Maybe next time, all right?"

Johanna nodded and waved as they drove off. She quickly turned into her gate, letting it slam behind her. She felt like slamming all kinds of things, doors, kettles. Her life here would be so perfect if it weren't for the sheriff—and her hungry heart.

By the end of the week, her skirt sagged at her middle. Johanna knew she better force herself to eat, but how did one turn off the thoughts and nightmares that followed the few times she had fallen asleep?

The days lapsed into weeks with Johanna sewing, fitting, and acting as if all were right. Inside she alternated between freezing and flaming.

One typical morning Henry woke her to say that Angel was crying. She leaped out of bed, remorse lending strength to her feet. If she couldn't even take care of her baby, what was going to happen to her? She had spent a fitful night and the nightmare she'd just released returned with a vengeance as she nursed a now smiling Angel. Raymond, always Raymond, pursuing her, this time with a whip. She could hear him rattling the door of her mind, no matter how hard he slammed it.

She finally made breakfast, cleaned up the kitchen, and sat down at her sewing machine. The dress for Clara had to be done today, she'd been at it far too long. Scolding herself for the miserable way she was acting had become a habit. When the bell tinkled to announce a customer, she pushed herself to her feet, squared her shoulders, and plastered a smile on her face.

The smile ran into hiding as soon as she saw the man standing in the middle of the shop. Summoning up every bit of strength she possessed, she forced herself to speak. "Good morning, Sheriff Stensrude, how can I help you this morning?"

He studied her face a moment before clearing his throat.

Henry, with Sam on his heels, darted through the curtained door and threw himself at Caleb's knees. The dog yipped and wagged, turning himself inside-out with joy.

Johanna flinched from another arrow of guilt. Sam was Caleb's dog, not theirs.

Caleb, blinking extra-fast, picked Henry up so he could look him right in the eye. "How've you been, son, taking good care of your ma?" Henry nodded so hard his hair flopped in the breeze. "I see Sam is in fine fettle, you been taking good care of him for me, huh?" Again Henry nodded. Caleb leaned over and sat the boy down, giving the dog a good ear rubbing at the same time. "Why don't you two go play in the other room, I need to talk with your ma."

Henry's shoulders slumped and his smile melted away but he did as told, only looking over his shoulder once before trudging out. He had buried his hand in Sam's ruff so the dog paced beside him.

Caleb turned his hat brim round and round in front of him. "I—hear you've been real busy." He cleared his throat—again.

"Ja, that I have." She memorized his face for the lonely nights.

"I—I come for my dog. I thought by this time Henry would be okay without him." His words came out in a rush as if he needed to get them over with.

Johanna nodded. "I've been telling him this day would come."

"I hate to do this to him but. . ." His words trailed off. He stared into her eyes, as if probing her soul.

Tell him he can come calling again. No, don't. The war exploded in her head.

"I'll get him for you." She tore her eyes from his and spun around. Ducking through the curtain, she wished she could do anything but this. She knelt in front of Henry, hands on his shoulders. "Son, you have to be very brave now, like we been talking about. Sheriff Stensrude needs Sam back."

A tear welled out of his blue eyes and sparkled on his cheek before being chased down by another.

Johanna fought the moisture gathering at the back of her throat and eyes. "You are such a good, big boy. I promise you, as soon as we hear of someone who has pups, we'll get one for you. That'll be your own dog."

Henry buried his face in the dog's fur, his shoulders shaking.

Sam turned and licked the tears off Henry's face, whining his sympathy.

"Come, Henry." She gave him her hand and together they walked into the shop, Sam padding beside the boy. "Thank you for loaning us your dog, Sheriff. We're much obliged."

"Johanna, I. . ."

"Goodbye, Sheriff." She turned and walked with Henry back to the kitchen where she sat in the rocker and lifted him into her lap. Finally the doorbell signaled his departure. Henry's sobs finally turned to sniffles but he remained leaning against her chest. The kitchen seemed empty.

When the bell tinkled again, she wished she had pulled down the closed sign. With a sigh, she deposited Henry on the floor and returned to the shop. "Gudrun, what a nice surprise."

"Hello, my dear. I'm sorry I've been so long without visiting you." She leaned on her knob-headed cane. "What has happened to you? You look terrible."

Johanna smoothed back her hair and sighed. "It's a long story."

"I have plenty of time to listen."

Johanna shook her head. "Not today. I don't think I'm up to it right now." She bit her lip at the compassion radiating from her friend. She felt guilty again. After all, she should have called on her when she knew the older woman wasn't feeling well. What kind of a friend was she?

Gudrun nodded. "Tomorrow then, you will come for dinner after church and when the children are down for their naps, we will get to the bottom of all this."

"I can't, I. . ."

"Caleb will not be invited."

"He—he came for Sam today."

"I'm so sorry." Gudrun squared her shoulders. "I will see you tomorrow then."

"Ja, we will come." When the old woman turned to leave, Johanna asked, "Did you need something today?"

Gudrun paused. "Yes, but we will deal with this other first. 'Til tomorrow then."

Johanna followed her to make sure there was no problem with the steps but Mrs. Norgaard sailed out the yard and to her waiting carriage, ignoring the mud caused by the melting snow. Johanna lifted her face to the sun's warmth. It had seemed clouds had covered the sun for the last month. Or was it only cloudy over her?

Each night and nap, Henry cried himself to sleep. Johanna stared down at him, shaking her head. Surely someone must have some puppies soon. She'd have to remember to ask Dag if he knew of any.

Sunday morning came rushing on like a runaway train. Every other minute she swore she would not go, not to church, not to Clara's, not outside her front door. In the saner minutes, she dressed the children for church and her-self too.

Ingeborg Moen met them at the door. "Oh, Johanna, I am so glad to see you. I've missed you but I couldn't even come calling because we've had the measles at our house and I didn't want to bring it to your children." She cooed at Angel and patted Henry on the head.

"Are they all right now?"

"Still some spots but back to running around so on the mend. Mary stayed home with them so I could come to church. I feel like I've been gone forever." She turned as the organ began to play. "Why don't you come sit with me, that all right with you, Henry?" At his nod, she added. "So there, that's all settled."

Since they sat in the front of the church, Johanna couldn't look around for Caleb. But she knew he wasn't there, she couldn't feel his presence. Though the service went by in a blur, one verse from the Gospel stayed with her: Jesus prom-ised to be a husband to the widows and a father to the fa-therless. *If only that applied to me.* She caught her thought in horror. She couldn't wish Raymond dead, no matter how much she feared him. It wasn't Christian.

After the service, she stood by Clara and Dag as he helped Mrs. Norgaard up in the carriage. He assisted the other two women aboard and lifted Henry up on the seat beside the driver. "If you think you're strong enough, you could maybe help me drive the team." The child's answering grin nearly broke his mother's heart. *As if it weren't in tatters already,* Johanna's mind responded.

When Dag lifted the boy onto his lap and invited him to take the reins with his own over them, light beamed from the boy's face.

"He'll make a good father, won't he?" Clara whispered.

"Very good," Johanna whispered back.

During the meal, swallowing small bites took every bit of concentration she possessed. She'd known from the look on Mrs. Olson's face that she would not tolerate food returning to the kitchen on Johanna's plate. Even so, she slipped some over to Henry's in the guise of cutting up his meat. Dag winked at her when she looked up, sending a rush of moisture to her eyes. Yelling she could handle, kindness no.

Later, after nursing Angel and putting both children down to sleep, she made her way back downstairs and into the parlor. Clara sat in front of the tall windows, her embroidery hoop in hand while Dag snored gently beneath the newspaper.

"She's in her office, waiting for you." She smiled at the look of trepidation that crossed Johanna's face. "She won't eat you, you know, and if you want me to come in and hold your hand, I will."

Johanna squared her shoulders. "No, thank you. I will manage. You can ask her later what happened." Clara nodded.

Johanna tapped at the door and, on invitation, entered the room. A fire crackled in the fireplace, throwing a rosy glow over the woman in the chair. The younger woman crossed and rubbed her frozen hands in the welcome heat before taking the other chair.

"Now, my dear, how can I help you?"

The warm tone made Johanna blink several times. She sighed. "I guess I will start at the beginning."

"That is always a good place."

"First of all, I am a married woman, not a widow like you probably surmised. I ran away from my husband because . . .because I couldn't stand his beatings anymore. I lost one other baby when he threw me against a wall and I was determined to not lose this one. . .Angel."

"And he beat Henry too?"

Johanna nodded. "I know that's why he doesn't talk. He did everything he could to become invisible. For years I thought it was all my fault, if I could try harder, be nicer, whatever, he would love me like he said he did in the beginning. My folks thought he was a fine man, they encouraged me to marry him and I agreed. I had a good, warm house, our farm produced well, what more could I ask for?"

"Did they know about his temper?"

"One day I told my mother but she said many men smacked their wives around a bit."

"A bit?"

"I never again told her how bad it was. When he broke my arm, I decided I couldn't stay any longer but it took months before I could leave. He watched me like a hawk." She looked down at her hands clenched in her lap, the knuckles white. "I've been so afraid he would come find me." Silence reigned for a time.

"That is why you sent Caleb away."

"Yes." The one word held all the misery locked in her trembling body.

Gudrun nodded. "I thought as much." She looked over the tops of her wire-rimmed glasses. "For I'm certain you love him, as he loves you."

"Yes. I thought I could just start anew, I've read stories of others who have done so, but I couldn't lie to him. How could I take more wedding vows when I am already married?" Johanna huddled into the back of her chair. "What do you think I should do?"

"I wish I knew, my dear, I just wish I knew."

eighteen

Dear God, I cannot go back, please, please don't make me go back, Johanna prayed silently as she leaned against the chair, grateful for its strength to uphold her. Surely God wouldn't ask such a thing of her, surely He wouldn't. She let her mind wander.

Raymond hadn't started to strike her until. . . She tried to think back. Was it after Henry was born? He'd been a colicky baby and many nights even her pacing the floor with him hadn't stopped his wails. Raymond roared that he needed his sleep if he were to harvest in the morning.

At first she excused his fits, knowing he was exhausted and worried about getting the harvest in before the rains came. Then it was because he'd had too much too drink one night at a neighbor's house. Finally, she knew it was all her fault, that nothing was ever done right, according to Raymond. The night he tipped over the highchair with Henry in it, to get to her, was the night he kicked her when she fell. She felt those bruises for weeks, mentally tasted the blood from the split lip, and remembered hardly seeing out of a blackened eye. He grew more violent as the months passed. Surely God wouldn't make her and her children leave the safety they had found and return to that life.

Gudrun sighed, bringing Johanna back to the present.

"I think we can only pray on this for the time being. Surely God has a plan in mind, but so far we just don't know what it is. Have you thought about what your options are?"

Johanna nodded. "I can stay or go back. Either way Caleb

148

will be out of my life." The thought weighed like a sack of wheat with fear nibbling a hole in the corner.

"I wonder if it wouldn't be a good thing to tell Caleb the entire story."

"I—I couldn't."

"Do you want me to?"

Johanna shook her head and shook it again. "No!" She paused. "No."

"He might have a good idea. . ."

"Gudrun, there is no law against beating your wife, she's a man's property to do with as he pleases, you know that."

"Thank God my Horace didn't believe that way, I don't know what I would have done." Silence again.

This time Johanna heard no voices from the past. Her little house and her growing business, they were hers and worth fighting for. If Caleb and her love for him were to be the sacrifice, so be it. Surely if Raymond were searching for her, he'd have come by now, before spring plowing began. He must have given up.

"Thank you for listening to me."

"Humph, near as I can see, I about twisted your arm off to get you here and talking." Gudrun made to rise. "I promise you, God will reveal His will in His good time. I've never known Him to fail."

Johanna quickly banished a recurring thought. *Why had God allowed such cruelty in the first place?*

Knowing that someone else shared her burden made the days lighter. Each evening Johanna took a few minutes to look in God's Word for His promises of protection. They were there but so were verses telling wives to submit to their husbands. She finished garments and started on newly commissioned ones. She made her first payment at the bank, feeling one step closer to owning the shop free and clear.

One afternoon, after Dag hung a swing from the oak branch for Henry, for the first time Henry discovered the joy of being pushed into the air. Since the weather was warmer, he played outside much of the time. One day she heard a yip and went to the window to see Sam charging through the opened gate and over to the boy. Caleb waited for him at the street, leaning backward against the fence post as if he couldn't bear even to look at her house.

He must hate her. Or not care anymore.

Wasn't that what she wanted? Him to stop caring and her heart to mend?

A few days later she put the children in the red wagon and walked over to the mansion, pulling the wagon behind her. Mrs. Olson greeted them with cries of delight.

"Clara, look who's here. Go tell Gudrun. Come in, come in, the coffee will be ready in a jiffy." She took the smiling baby from Johanna and, after hugging her and planting a kiss on the rosy cheek, carried her into the kitchen, talking all the while.

When Clara returned she hugged Johanna and stooped down in front of Henry. "How's my favorite boy today? Brought your wagon, I see." Henry nodded, eyes bright and a smile showing off the dimple in his cheek. "I think Mrs. Olson has cookies in the cookie jar, but if I get you one, you won't tell anyone, will you?" He shook his head, the grin even broader.

Gudrun, her cane bearing more of her weight than ever, tapped her way into the room and greeted them all. As soon as she sat down, she motioned Henry over. "Why, Henry, I think you've gotten all grown up since I saw you last." She cuddled him in the crook of her arm when Mrs. Olson leaned over to see Angel.

"Ain't she just the purtiest?"

"Lives up to her name, that's for certain." She reached up and took the baby onto her lap. Angel gurgled and cooed, waving her arms and kicking her feet free of the blanket.

"She's getting to be a handful to hold nowadays. She wants to keep up with Henry already." Johanna sat down across the table. "She thinks riding in that wagon and seeing the world is the greatest thing since the wheel was invented. The streets are finally dry enough we don't sink up to our ankles in the gumbo."

"Have you started your garden yet?" Clara asked, taking another chair and drawing Henry to her.

"I've gotten some digging done but the sewing keeps me so busy, I don't know how to do it all."

"Why don't we send Frank over to spade it up for her?" Mrs. Olson set the coffee cups in front of them and a platter with cake and cookies both on the table.

"It's too small to bring a horse in to plow it, or I'd have asked Dag if he knew someone who would do that."

"Well, don't you worry, another couple of days and Frank can take a break here and help you." Gudrun looked up from talking with the baby. "I think she understands every word we say."

The words Johanna really wanted to hear were about Caleb but she couldn't bring herself to ask any questions about him. Strange how in a town so small, they didn't run into each other at all. Perhaps he was being as careful to stay away as she. "Thank you, I would surely appreciate the help."

They chatted about the goings-on of Soldahl but no mention was made of Caleb. When Johanna got to her feet, saying it was time for them to head on home, Clara volunteered to walk partway with her. Mrs. Olson tucked a packet of things she'd been collecting into the wagon.

"Just for your supper, nothing much." She hugged Henry, smacked a last kiss on Angel's cheek, and handed her to her mother. "You don't wait so long to come back, you hear?"

"I won't." They waved good-bye and started down the walk. Clara pointed out the tips of the tulips and daffodils peeking from the ground and they laughed at a squirrel scampering up a tree. Clara turned into the blacksmith shop with a wave good-bye and the others continued on to the little house set back from the street.

That evening when she was at her sewing machine again, Johanna thought back to the day. For the first time since her marriage, she had friends, true friends who cared what happened to her. What a pleasure it would be to have a man dig up the garden for her. Later she found herself humming a tune in time with the treadle.

Sunday her heart leaped nearly out of her breast when she saw Caleb sitting in a pew, second from the rear. Ingeborg invited her down front to sit with her and her finally recovered brood so she made her way up the center aisle. Her back felt as if two smoldering coals were laid side by side on it. When would the sight of him not affect her so strongly? Nightly she'd prayed to be delivered from the love she felt for him. And just when she thought she was on the mend, this happened.

Mary asked to take Angel so Johanna held Henry on her lap instead. He peeked out around her shoulder at the antics of one of the young Moen boys, whose mother kept shushing and sending threatening glances. Once Henry giggled. His mother hugged him close, grateful for any sound he made. Perhaps one day he would talk again, now that he felt safe.

Reverend Moen based his sermon on the tale of Onesimus, the slave Paul told to go back to his master. Each word bit into Johanna's heart. Was God saying she had to go back? By the end of the sermon, she felt sure. A calm settled over her, and she squared her shoulders and her will. If God demanded this, surely He would give her the strength to carry it out. What would she do when she got there? All she knew was if this were the price of peace of mind, steep though it was, she believed God knew what He was doing.

He was telling her to go back to Wisconsin.

"You've decided, haven't you?" Gudrun walked out with her.

"How do you know?"

"The answer is in your face, my dear. Now we must work out how to do this great deed."

"We?"

"You did not think we would leave you to fight this battle alone?" Gudrun shook her head. "No, that's what friends are for, to share a burden."

"But—but you've been ill and. . ."

"And you think I'm too weak for such a trip?"

"No—yes—I don't know." She looked down in time to see Henry dart across the grass. He flung himself at the sheriff's legs and his face nearly cracked in two when Caleb picked him up. The two hugged each other, the boy disappearing in the strong arms of the man.

Gudrun followed her gaze. "Those two are a pair, are they not?"

"Yes, they are." If only she dared to do the same.

"Back to our discussion. When would you like to leave?"

Johanna tore her gaze from the man and child and returned to Gudrun. "As soon as I have the money for the train fare."

"If that's all, we can leave tomorrow. Henry will stay at our house. Of course he will be spoiled rotten by the time we return. Since you are still nursing, Angel will have to go with us."

"I—I. . ." Johanna now knew what it felt like to be caught in a tornado and spun around, all out of control. "I have two orders that have to be finished first. Gudrun, I cannot keep taking charity from you like this."

"Call it a loan then. You can pay me back when you can."

Clara came to stand beside them. "What have I been missing?"

"Johanna and I are leaving for Wisconsin on Thursday." She smiled at Johanna. "That will give you time, right?"

The younger woman nodded. She couldn't have spoken if her life depended on it.

"Good." Clara reached for Angel. "Please let me hold her for a bit. I need to get some practice in." She turned as Caleb came up to them, Henry on his shoulders, both hands lodged in Caleb's hair.

"Isn't she beautiful, Caleb? She's growing so fast." Clara held tightly to the squirming baby. "I think she wants to get down and run with the other children. Won't be long now, will it, sweet thing?" Angel gurgled and cooed back, her arms and feet going as if she were already on the ground and running.

Caleb reached a finger to touch the baby's face. She grabbed on and pulled it into her mouth, slobbering and gumming it as if it were the greatest treat.

"Ouch." He pulled back. "She's got teeth."

"No, she doesn't." Johanna said with a smile.

"You want to bet?" Caleb pried open the baby's mouth. "See, right there." A flash of white glowed against the pink gums.

"Her first tooth." Johanna took a hankie from her pocket and wiped Angel's chin. "I hope she didn't hurt you." She looked up at him from under her lashes.

"I'll live. I have something for Henry. Is it all right if I bring it by this afternoon?"

"Of course."

"See you later, son." He sat the boy down beside his mother, tipped his hat to the women, and strode off, greeting others as he went.

Johanna laid a hand on her son's shoulder, keeping him by her side, when she knew all he wanted was to dart after the sheriff. His eyes said it all. He missed Caleb about as much as she did.

"I will check the train schedule and let you know what time we leave. Mrs. Olson will fix us a basket of food—she never lets anyone leave without being heartily prepared—and we will be on our way."

"You ladies about ready to go home?" Dag called from the buggy he pulled up by the end of the walk.

Gudrun nodded. "If there is anything you need, you ask, all right?" She peered over her spectacles at Johanna, waiting for an answer.

When Johanna finally nodded, Gudrun took her by the arm. "Come, we will give you a ride home."

Later that afternoon a knock on the door brought both her and Henry to see who it was. Caleb stood on the porch, an open box in his arms and Sam by his side.

"We brought this little guy for Henry, to kind of replace Sam. Since Sam is the pa, I thought that might make him even more welcome." He squatted down with the box so Henry could see and looked up at her. "It's all right, isn't it? I know I should have asked you first but. . ."

"It's fine, Sheriff. I've been meaning to get him a dog soon as we heard of someone who had a litter."

Henry dropped on his knees beside the box. He stroked the wriggling puppy's head and ducked when Sam gave him a quick lick.

"You can hold him." Caleb read the plea in the boy's eyes. "He's eight weeks old and already been trained to eat solid food. 'Fraid he's not housebroken though, but he should learn quick, if he's anything like his pa." He gave Sam a thump on the ribs.

Henry picked the puppy up and snuggled him under his chin. The puppy licked every bit of bare skin he could reach and then repeated the measure. Henry looked up at his mother who nodded, and then over at the sheriff, and back at the puppy. The grin he wore scrunched his eyes nearly closed and his infectious giggle left Johanna heartbroken.

"Thank you, Caleb."

Caleb got to his feet. "Johanna, we have to talk."

"I know. Gudrun and I are leaving on the train on Thursday and when I return I will tell you everything." She knew she'd return if for no other reason than to close her shop and retrieve Henry.

"I will wait." He bent down to Henry. "You take good care of that little one now, you hear. He's your dog, not your ma's." Henry nodded, his eyes round. "Good, then I must be going." Caleb tipped his hat, patted Henry on the shoulder, and strode off down the walk.

Johanna sighed. What was it she would be telling him?

nineteen

The clacking of the rails lulled Angel to sleep.

"She's getting to be a busy one, isn't she?" Gudrun asked from the seat across the private room. She had insisted on such accommodations, saying that Angel needed space to play on the floor or her mother would be exhausted by the time they reached Wisconsin. And so would she. If only she could nod off so easily, Johanna thought wistfully. The last few days had been a nightmare what with trying to finish the existing orders, not take any new ones, and mop up after the puppy, now dubbed Samson. The frisky fellow still hadn't quite got the hang of asking to go out. She knew it wasn't Henry's fault. He kept Samson outside with him much of the day. They had claimed a corner of the garden Frank dug up and were busy digging a hole. No matter how hard she tried to convince the boy that until the puppy was housebroken, he had to sleep on the back porch, she would find the pup, snuggled right under Henry's arm, on her son's bed.

She smiled when she remembered the horrified look on Mrs. Olson's face when they arrived, puppy in tow. But right away she'd fixed a box behind the kitchen stove. Johanna was willing to bet that Henry would be found sleeping back there or the puppy would end up in his bed every night they were there.

She looked over at Gudrun whose head was bobbing drowsily. "Why don't you lie down on the seat and let me cover you with the quilt?" she whispered so as not to disturb Angel.

The old woman blinked awake. She covered a yawn with her gloved hand. "I think I will at that. I'd forgotten how lulling a train ride can be."

Johanna reached up into the overhead compartment for a pillow to go along with the quilt. They had brought their own when Mrs. Olson had a fit at the thought of her friends using those provided by the train. After all, who knew who had used them last?

When the old woman was settled, Johanna wrapped the other quilt around her shoulders and lay down herself. Better to sleep while and if she could. Who knew how well Angel would be behaving by nightfall?

They changed trains in Fargo and then again in St. Paul. They were due to arrive at Hammerville, Wisconsin, before first light. Every clack of the wheels reminded Johanna of the trip she'd made west in December, the weeks of running, always fearful of Raymond tracking them. She shuddered at the thought. Her, big as a house, and Henry plastered against her side, terrified of every sound.

Johanna had all their things repacked and ready at the door when the conductor announced their stop as one after the next. Angel still lay asleep. Johanna thanked the Lord for the favor and repinned her hat in place.

Dawn had only cracked the dark when they stepped onto the station platform. Johanna looked around, feeling as if she had stepped into a different world. She'd come here once with the wagon to pick up machinery that Raymond had ordered but was too busy to pick up. After the train pulled out, she could hear a dog bark in the distance and the familiar crowing of a rooster.

Hammerville, what would they find here? Even the sound of the name brought back painful memories.

"I believe we will go to the hotel first, if we can get the station master to carry our things." Gudrun looked around and started toward the lighted window in the station building. "Then we can have breakfast there, leave our things in the rooms, and order a buggy for the trip to the farm. How long did you say it would take?"

"About an hour, depends on the roads."

"Good, we should be there by noon, easily." She crossed the platform, her heels clicking on the worn boards. Before Johanna had time to disagree, if she had the nerve, they were ensconced in a large room with two beds at the hotel and the maid had gone to find a crib, in spite of the mother's disagreement. Even she could tell that what Gudrun said was law.

After Angel nursed and fell back asleep Johanna crawled under the covers and stretched out. While her body loved the warmth and settled in, her mind went winging across the land. What would they find when they reached the farm? Had Raymond divorced her? Would he attack in a rage because she had left? What would she do?

Father in heaven, I am counting on You, she prayed fervently. *You brought us this far, You must have a plan. You took care of the Israelites crossing the desert and protected Your people from so many enemies. Please guard us now. Amen.* And then a fussing Angel woke her up.

Her mouth grew drier the closer they got to the farm. She recognized the house of their neighbors, knowing that their fence line was half a mile away, the house and barns half a mile beyond that.

"Are you all right?" Gudrun asked, looking over the head of the child she held on her lap.

"Ja, I will be." Johanna clucked the horse to a faster trot. All within her wanted to turn the buggy around and head back for town and the train west. She slowed and guided the horse left into the long driveway.

Funny, the front fields weren't plowed yet. Had they had such a nasty spring that Raymond couldn't get out in the fields? Perhaps he was plowing the back section first. She pulled the horse to a stop and looked around before driving up to the house.

There were no cows in the pasture, no dog barking in greeting. Indeed the house wore the look of no one home. No smoke arose from the chimney, and the gate to the yard was hanging open.

She turned to look at Gudrun who raised her shoulders in question. Where had he gone? She pulled the horse to a stop at the gate and, after wrapping the reins around the whip stock, stepped down. "You wait for me here."

The door was locked. She peeked in the window. Everything looked the same, the red and white oilcloth on the table, four chairs pulled up to it. Then she noticed that the banking hadn't been removed from around the foundation. Raymond always used the old straw and manure to cover the garden before he plowed it.

She shaded her eyes, looking across the fields. Nothing had been done.

When she climbed back in the buggy, she shook her head. "I don't know," she answered before Gudrun could ask the question. "Guess we'll go back to the Tengsvolds and ask." She turned the buggy around and clucked the horse forward. As soon as they reached the road, she flapped the reins, making the horse go into a trot.

Where had Raymond gone and when had he left?

"My land, look who's here." Mrs. Tengsvold threw open the door before Johanna could even knock. "Oh, my dear, I am so happy to see you. And you have someone with you?"

She waved and raised her voice. "Come in, come in. Dinner is nearly ready."

Johanna thanked her and returned to the buggy for Angel and to help Mrs. Norgaard down. Together they walked back to the porch.

"And this is your baby? Isn't she a wonder?" She reached out to take Gudrun's hand as Johanna introduced them. "Oh, I am so glad you are all right. Why, we thought maybe you died in the snow last winter or. . ." All the while she talked she brought her guests in the house and helped remove their coats. "You just take a place at the table now and. . ."

"Mrs. Tengsvold, Elmira, what has happened to Raymond? The farm is vacant." Johanna interrupted the woman's chatter.

"I know. It was a sad thing." She sank down on a chair and took Johanna's free hand in hers. "Bjorn didn't see the smoke in the chimney for a couple of mornings so he thought he better check on you folks. When he got there, the house was empty, so he checked the barn. We didn't know what had happened to you of course."

"Yes."

"Well, he found your husband lying in the bull's pen. He'd been gored and stomped to death. There was a big cut in the bull's side but he was doing all right. Fair to dying for a drink of water though. With the broken pitchfork and all, we didn't know if he were beating the bull off or what. I'm so sorry, we didn't have any idea how to let you know. Bjorn said we would just have to wait. He brought the livestock over here. We was hoping you would come back sometime." Her words finally ran out.

Johanna couldn't find her voice. She knew she should feel sad but all she could think was *Thank You, God, thank You, thank You.* She shouldn't be grateful for a man's death, and a violent one at that. All this time she'd worried about him finding her. And he'd been dead. She buried her face in Angel's neck, the tears starting in spite of her iron will.

"Now, now, I know the shock is hard to take."

"Who's the company?" Bjorn Tengsvold called from the backdoor. "Dinner ready yet?"

"In a minute." Elmira bustled back to the stove after another pat on Johanna's shoulder.

"Well, look who's here! You are all right, I'm so glad." A smile wreathed his face turned ruddy from hours in the sun. In few strides he crossed the room in his stocking feet, having left his dirty boots at the backdoor. He looked to his wife at the stove. "I see you told her."

He dropped into the chair at the head of the table. "It was such a shock to us too. Nothing we could do but bury him when the ground thawed out enough."

"Where?" Johanna wiped her eyes and jiggled Angel on her lap.

"In the cemetery behind the Lutheran church. I know you didn't go much but I—we thought it best. We put a gravestone on it so's you could find it, if'n you ever came back."

The enormity of what had happened was more than she could take in.

"We locked up the house, brought your livestock over here. When I saw that old horse was gone, I had an idea what had happened." He ducked his head. "We—ah—had an idea what had been going on, but you know Raymond. So privatelike, didn't seem nothing we could do."

"No, there wasn't. I thank you for what you did." So, he'd beaten the bull once too often. Ever since she'd raised the tiny calf when he planned to club it, he'd had it in for the animal. When it threw good calves the animal seemed to goad him even more. She could about picture what had happened. When Raymond found her gone, he took his anger and frustration out on the animal. But this time was the final straw.

When the two strapping Tengsvold sons came in, Elmira set the food on the table and, after grace, urged everyone to eat up. They peppered Johanna with questions about her life in Soldahl, how Henry was, if he were talking now.

"Landsakes, how's she supposed to eat with all you badgering her?" Elmira's voice strained to be heard.

"Sorry, sorry," the boys said.

"You go ahead and eat while I ask you one more question." Bjorn Tengsvold looked directly at Johanna. "Now if you want to come back and farm that piece, we'll help you all we can, but if you want to sell it, Nils here is prepared to buy. He wants to get married and this will give him a starting place. We'll take all the livestock, furniture, whatever you want to leave."

"I—I don't know. This is all so sudden." Johanna looked to Gudrun who barely nodded her head. Johanna sipped her coffee, her dinner forgotten in front of her. "I really need to go back over there."

"Understandable. I'll give you the key."

"Could I give you my decision tomorrow?"

"Of course, of course, no need to rush. Just that those fields need to get worked up soon as possible if we want a crop off them this fall."

"I know." Angel chose that moment to whimper for her meal. "Could I use your bedroom to feed her?"

"Surely." Elmira jumped to her feet. "Right this way. I'll put your plate on to warm for you."

Johanna sat in a chair by the window, alternating between looking out at the fields and down at her baby. Should she bring her children back here so Henry could eventually have his father's farm, if he wanted it? Did she want to leave her cozy home and busy shop to live back out in the country, a mile away from the nearest neighbor? She could hear Gudrun visiting with the Tengsvolds. There were two things she knew she must do: return to the house and go to the cemetery. Everything else could wait.

With Elmira waving them on their way and Angel sound asleep in Gudrun's lap, Johanna turned the buggy around and headed back to the silent farm.

The stale smell of the empty house assaulted her when she opened the door. She walked to the stove and thought about starting a fire to burn the smell away but she decided against it. Instead she walked to the bedroom where she had cowered so many times. Raymond's pants still lay over the back of the chair, waiting for her to patch them. With a swift move, she jerked the quilt her mother had given her off the bed and folded it, picked up her Bible and her sewing basket, and returned to the kitchen. A quick look around confirmed what she already knew. There was nothing else she wanted.

"That's all you want?" Gudrun asked when she returned to the buggy.

"Ja, that's it. I hope young Tengsvold and his new wife will be far happier here than we were. It is good farmland. One thing to be said for Raymond, he took good care of the land and the livestock—except for the bull. Do you suppose one day I will have room in my heart to forgive him?"

"You mean your husband or the bull?"

"It was a hard way to die." She unwound the reins and turned the horse around. "I warned him again and again not to treat the bull that way. Was this justice, do you think?"

"I can't answer that. Where to now?"

"The Tengsvolds. I don't want to come back here ever again."

"Do you think Henry might want the farm someday? You could rent it to them, you know."

"I thought of that but Henry has no good memories of this place either. Better that he not have to make a decision. I wonder what a farm goes for here now?" She clucked the horse into a trot.

After agreeing to meet Bjorn and his son at the bank in the morning, she and Gudrun headed back to town. The Lutheran church lay a couple of miles up the road, its cross-crowned steeple glinting above the trees.

Birds sang in the fenced-in cemetery and a butterfly flitted from the branches of the apple tree that grew by the gate. Bees hummed about their business in the blossoms. Johanna dismounted from the buggy and entered the grassy yard, looking at the headstones until she came upon a fairly fresh grave. There was no inscription, only his name and the year of death. She stared at it, waiting for some feeling of any kind to make itself known. *Ah, Raymond, we started our life together with such high hopes and look what it has come to.* As she dashed away the one tear that meandered down her cheek, she pulled a pigweed out of the dirt oblong and flung it over the fence.

On the way back to the hotel they stopped by the livery and paid the fee and a boy hopped on the back of the buggy so he could return it to the barn. Supper and an early bed were all Johanna wanted.

Her first thought in the morning shocked her wide awake. *I'm free. I no longer have to be afraid.* Then guilt dropped a load on her shoulders. *I should be sad, grieving for my husband. Lord, what is wrong with me?* She lay in bed and thought of her new life in Soldahl. Surely God had led her there as He protected her from death in the blizzard. Surely He held her in His hand. *God is my strength and salvation.* She repeated it for good measure. *Please, Father, give me wisdom for this day. Thank You for Your many blessings.*

She glanced at the crib where Angel slept, knees tucked under her, bottom in the air. Such a blessing. Then she began counting all her blessings, trying hard not to wiggle so the creaking bed would waken her sleeping friend. Gudrun, how many lives had she blessed with her mind and her wealth? Some time later, when she had finally run out of things to be thankful for, she could no longer remain in bed.

Dressing behind the screen in the corner, she took her soap and towel to the bathroom at the end of the hall. By the time she returned, Angel was yawning and stretching and Gudrun dressing behind the screen.

"Would you like me to go to the bank with you or stay here and watch Angel?" Gudrun asked over the rim of her coffee cup. They were seated at a table for four in the dining room and Angel, in a highchair chased bits of toast around the wooden tray. Johanna had fed the baby a few bites of oatmeal and egg.

"You know much more about contracts than I do. Why don't you go to the bank and I'll stay with Angel?" Johanna smiled at the slow shaking of Gudrun's head. "No? Then how about if we go together and I'll play with Angel while you read the papers over for me?"

"How much are you going to ask for the farm?"

"I'm going to see how much they offer, raise it some, and sign the papers. We should be able to make the afternoon train."

And so they did. A couple of times during the ride west, Johanna took the check out of her bag to make sure it was real. She could pay off her shop and have money left to put in the bank. Never had she felt so wealthy. Never had the cost been greater.

"And to think I almost didn't come."

"I know. But remember, we prayed for God's guidance. He never wants us to live in fear and this is how He took care of yours. Now we must pray for Henry, to put this all behind him."

"He still has nightmares but not nearly so often. They came back for a while after Caleb took Sam home but now he seems at peace again. Poor little fellow."

When the train pulled into Soldahl, Caleb met her on the platform.

"What are you—how did you know—?" Her words vanished at the look on his face.

"I've met every train so I wouldn't miss you." He helped Gudrun down first. "How was your trip?" He took their bags and put them off to the side.

"I will tell you about it later." Johanna's smile brought forth one from him.

"Come on, ladies, I will drive you home."

twenty

"Johanna, will you marry me?" His words echoed through the darkness.

Crickets sang over by the fence. A mosquito whined in her ear. Johanna stared up at the moon glowing like a huge silver platter. In the shade of the oak tree, she couldn't really see his face, just a form lighter than the surrounding shadows.

"Yes, but. . ."

"But what?" He covered her hands with his on the swing.

"But it can't be until after the time of grieving." She forced the words past the lump in her throat.

"Grieving! He wasn't worth grieving for! Besides, Raymond died nearly six months ago. That's long enough." Johanna had told him the entire story as she promised the first night they were back.

"But Caleb, what will people say?"

"Who cares? Only the Moens along with those at Dag's house know what happened anyway, and they won't tell." He jiggled the swing, making her bounce. "I think we've waited long enough."

His rich voice sent shivers racing up and down her spine. She slapped at the pesky mosquito. "All right, when?" She couldn't believe those words came from her.

"Next Saturday."

"That's only four days away." She squeaked on the last words.

"No, a week from this Saturday."

"That's too soon, I think maybe June."

"A week from Saturday." He picked her up from the swing seat and held her to his chest. She wrapped her arms around his neck.

"You carried me once before."

"Lot easier this time." He set her down on the porch, down in the corner where the light from the window didn't reach. When their lips finally met, Johanna felt she'd come home.

"I won't have time to make a new dress," she said sometime later.

"I'm marrying you, not a dress. You'll look lovely no matter what you wear."

She rested her head against his chest. "You. . ." But he took her breath away with another kiss.

ᴥ

Saturday dawned bright and fair but by nine showers had arrived. Johanna shivered in the coolness. Rain on a wedding day, not a good thing. As if reading her thoughts, by noon the sun sparkled on drops left on leaves and grass blades.

"Come, your carriage awaits." Dag met her at the door and pointed to Clara and Gudrun with Mrs. Olson, sitting in the buggy. Dag and Clara had agreed to stand up with the bridal couple.

Johanna didn't have much to say. Her heart was beating so fast she half expected it to leap out of her chest and fly away. Henry climbed up on Clara's lap, Mrs. Olson took the baby, and Johanna wished she were walking or running away.

"Don't worry, my dear, all brides—and grooms—get the jitters on their wedding day. You'll be fine." Gudrun leaned forward and patted Johanna's knee.

"And we got food enough to feed the whole town back at the house. I baked the wedding cake myself." Mrs. Olson tickled Angel and made her chortle.

"You shouldn't have."

"Yes, we should." Clara handed Henry up to sit by Dag. "You just enjoy the day."

Oh yes, that's what she'd do, enjoy the day, if she didn't embarrass everybody, herself most of all. She laid a hand on her stomach to calm it. Whatever possessed her to agree to such a fast wedding?

At precisely one o'clock the organist looked toward the door and the old pipe organ broke into song. Clara walked down the aisle first, tulips from their garden in her arms. The excited congregation craned to look as Johanna stepped through the door. Were those tears she saw sparkling in Caleb's eyes? Tears to match those that threatened to spill over her own cheeks?

"Dearly beloved, we are gathered here in the sight of God and this holy gathering to bring these two people together in holy matrimony." Reverend Moen spoke the age-old words with joy and reverence. Both Caleb and Johanna answered in voices strong and sure, their eyes pledging their troth along with their voices.

"I now pronounce you man and wife. What God hast put together, let no man rend asunder." Then he leaned forward and whispered, "You may kiss the bride."

And Caleb did. As he and Johanna turned to make their way back up the aisle, Henry shot out of the pew and made a beeline for Caleb's pant leg. With Johanna's arm still in his, the man leaned down and picked up the boy, settling him into the crook of the other arm.

Johanna smiled up at him adoringly.

The little boy put his hands on either side of Caleb's face and turned it to face him. "My pa," he said, loud enough for most to hear. "My pa."

A Letter To Our Readers

Dear Reader:

In order that we might better contribute to your reading enjoyment, we would appreciate your taking a few minutes to respond to the following questions. When completed, please return to the following:

Rebecca Germany, Managing Editor
Heartsong Presents
P.O. Box 719
Uhrichsville, Ohio 44683

1. Did you enjoy reading *Dakota December*?
   ❑ Very much. I would like to see more books
     by this author!
   ❑ Moderately
     I would have enjoyed it more if _____
     _____

2. Are you a member of **Heartsong Presents**? ❑Yes ❑No
   If no, where did you purchase this book?_____
   _____

3. What influenced your decision to purchase this
   book? (Check those that apply.)

   ❑ Cover   ❑ Back cover copy

   ❑ Title   ❑ Friends

   ❑ Publicity   ❑ Other_____

4. How would you rate, on a scale from 1 (poor) to 5
   (superior), the cover design? _____

5. On a scale from 1 (poor) to 10 (superior), please rate the following elements.

    __Heroine   __Plot

    __Hero   __Inspirational theme

    __Setting   __Secondary characters

6. What settings would you like to see covered in **Heartsong Presents** books?_____

_____

_____

7. What are some inspirational themes you would like to see treated in future books?_____

_____

_____

8. Would you be interested in reading other **Heartsong Presents** titles?   ❏ Yes   ❏ No

9. Please check your age range:
  ❏ Under 18   ❏ 18-24   ❏ 25-34
  ❏ 35-45   ❏ 46-55   ❏ Over 55

10. How many hours per week do you read? _____

Name _____

Occupation _____

Address _____

City_____ State_____ Zip _____

Christmas Treasures

*Four new love stories
from Christmases past and present*

An Ozark Christmas Angel by **Veda Boyd Jones**
A sneaky matchmaker thinks Christmas would be
the perfect time for Lindsay and a certain doctor to fall in love.

Christmas Dream by **Tracie J. Peterson**
An Alaskan snowstorm grounds newlyweds Mark and Rita
Williams in the Juneau airport for their first Christmas together.

Winterlude by **Colleen L. Reece**
A single out-of-place snowflake in San Diego
lures Ariel Dixon to Ketchikan, Alaska,
home to a handsome childhood friend presumed dead.

Dakota Destiny by **Lauraine Snelling**
Two years after Mary received word
that Will is presumed dead in World War I,
she wants only to dream of his return.

(352 pages, Paperbound, 5" x 8")

Heartsong Presents
Love Stories Are Rated G!

That's for godly, gratifying, and of course, great! If you love a thrilling love story, but don't appreciate the sordidness of some popular paperback romances, **Heartsong Presents** is for you. In fact, **Heartsong Presents** is the *only inspirational romance book club*, the only one featuring love stories where Christian faith is the primary ingredient in a marriage relationship.

Sign up today to receive your first set of four, never before published Christian romances. Send no money now; you will receive a bill with the first shipment. You may cancel at any time without obligation, and if you aren't completely satisfied with any selection, you may return the books for an immediate refund!

Imagine. . .four new romances every four weeks—two historical, two contemporary—with men and women like you who long to meet the one God has chosen as the love of their lives. . .all for the low price of $9.97 postpaid.

To join, simply complete the coupon below and mail to the address provided. **Heartsong Presents** romances are rated G for another reason: They'll arrive *Godspeed!*